YOUNGER'S RACE

YOUNGER'S RACE

BY ELIZABETH ALLEN

A THISTLE BOOK
Published by

GROSSET & DUNLAP, INC.
A National General Company
New York

For my helpers, Bob and Jim
Also for Lilibet and Carlotta Allen

YOUNGER'S
RACE

Chapter One

TOM WALKED ALONG the hall of Hoover High with his head bent down. He'd been called into the office after school because of his grades, which was bad enough, but then they'd had trouble finding his file because his name was Hendricks and his mother's was Smythe. Warm air blew toward him from the open door, and he looked up. Soon it would be summer, he thought; Lion would be home and they'd go racing. That was something good to think about. He flipped his dark hair from his forehead, gave a sudden jump, and then ran outside.

Someone hit him. He went down. Then he heard a low laugh; it was Lion! Tom stuck out his foot to trip him and then rolled neatly aside as his brother fell flat.

"I've been waiting for you, Younger," Lion yelled. He picked himself up. "Where've you been?"

"I thought you were up at your college!"

"We're going racing tomorrow at Alvad. C'mon. I haven't even checked out Purple Haze yet."

"Tomorrow!"

Lion had started off, and Tom jumped to his feet and followed him through the empty parking lot of Hoover, past the ball diamond, across a field, and toward a narrow street. He caught up with Lion halfway down the road and they jogged along together. Their house, its angles of brick and wood stacked against a hill, was almost hidden by trees. The two ran up a driveway across a ravine to slam open the door of a garage. There was their drag car, Purple Haze.

"It still surprises me that it stands so high," Tom said. "After more than a year, it still does."

"It's modified! The front-end lift kit and the traction bars make it high. You know that!"

"Yeah." Tom ga-- the purple surface a slap. He especially liked the paint job, and you didn't see many purple cars around. It gave him a feeling of being near power and speed. "Someday we'll get the name on it."

Lion nodded. "In gold leaf. But that'll have to wait."

He was staring at the car intently and was probably, Tom thought, remembering all the hours he'd pumped gas to buy parts.

"Did you fire it at least once a week?" Lion asked.

"At least once. I can't do it much oftener; it scares everybody when you start it up."

"I know." He nodded and began circling the car. "Is everybody all right?" he asked, still circling. "You okay? Mom? Bonnie? Step?"

"Everyone's fine."

He had the hood up by then, and was peering into the engine. Lion could look very intense, and often reminded Tom of the guy in the movie walking into town to find the marshal. He had worn his brown hair short in high school, and his nickname had been Trains, but now he wore his hair long and bushy and was called Lion. It figured.

"We're really racing at Alvad?"

"Sure thing. You remember it; we've been there before."

Tom nodded. It was a small track, but a good one.

"Do you think we can get everything ready to-night?"

Lion nodded, his hair flapping, and then went over to the workbench where he kept his tools.

"Lion?" called a voice from above. It was their stepbrother, Robie, who lived in the big room above the garage.

"How are you doing, Step?" Lion called.

"I'm fine, thanks."

They heard a chair scrape, and footsteps coming down some stairs, and then a slight, somewhat stooped boy appeared at the back door. He smiled at them uncertainly as he poked at his glasses.

I don't know why Robie always looks at you as if he expected to get hit in the nose. It bothered Tom. *The guy ought to toughen up.*

"I'm getting ready for graduation and all, Lion," Robie said.

"Good, good." Lion didn't look up.

Tom glanced at Robie. "Hi."

"Hi ya, Younger."

Tom felt a flash of anger. Robie had a nerve, calling him Younger. Just because the guy was a senior instead of a junior he apparently considered himself much older, but actually there was only a few months' difference in their ages.

"There was a Progress Report in the mail for you." Robie was looking at him. "What are you flunking now?"

Tom decided to just overlook the remark. Robie was often in a bad mood. He started to reach for Lion's trouble-light on the wall.

"I'm surprised you even bother to go to school, dummered."

That was too much.

Tom started for Robie right through the screen door, but Lion said, in a low voice, "Hang loose." Tom stopped and turned around. The Chevy was coming up the long circular driveway, with his mother and their little half sister, Bonnie. He was glad he had stopped. Mom hated it when any of them got in a fight.

"Li-on!" It was Bonnie. She was out of the car almost before it came to a halt, running toward them with her long hair flying to wrap herself around Lion. "I thought you had to stay at your dorm and be a Proctor!"

"Hi ya, Bon Bon." Lion peeled her off his legs. "They didn't need me this weekend."

"Lionel!" Tom could hear their mother calling, as she parked in the paved circle that ended their driveway. "Come over here and give me a hug."

"I may have grease on me," Lion said, going over to her.

"I'm used to that."

"I got a hundred in spelling again!" Bonnie was now wrapped around Tom.

"Great." It was nice that somebody in the family had brains. He peeled her off.

"Have you seen my cat?" She ran off toward the ravine.

Lion had been talking to their mother, and now Tom heard him say that they were going racing.

"You are? Tomorrow? Saturday?"

She doesn't like us going, Tom thought, worried.

He turned to his mother.

"Do you have groceries or anything in the car, Mom?"

"Yes."

Just that and no more; "Yes." As he stood looking at her Lion grabbed the groceries and took them inside and then jumped back out the door and crawled under the Haze. He was a big help.

Tom followed his mother into the house. She looked up and shook her head, sighing. His mom had the dark hair and green eyes which he had inherited; a good combination for a woman, in his opinion, but wrong for a man.

"You aren't really bugged about our racing, are you?" he asked. "Drag racing under the National Hot Rod Association rules is safer than driving on the streets."

"So I've heard." She sighed.

"And we never go to an outlaw track. Never!"

"That's good."

She started toward her room. Tom trailed her through the living room and down the flight of steps to the hall.

"I promised," he heard her say, almost to herself.

He knew what she meant. She had been able to buy this house because it was on a forgotten-looking lane near a ravine people used as a dump, and when he and Lion had cleaned it up she'd been so pleased that she'd told Lion he could go ahead and build the racing car he'd been wanting to have all his life. "And race it, I guess," she had laughed. She'd had no idea that Lion would really be able to do what he'd done.

Tom turned a corner. This house, a split level, had almost too many floors, although it was about a hundred per cent better than any of the apartments they had lived in. He followed his mother into her bedroom. There was his father's picture on the dresser. It always gave him a jolt because, in spite of the haircut and the uniform, he looked so much like Lion. And his dad seemed so young; how could he be dead? But he was. He'd been killed in Korea; he had gone away and not come back. *I never knew him.*

"Tom, would you mind not jumping around like that?"

He hadn't realized he'd been doing it.

"Sorry. Bad day downtown?"

"Well, we were busy."

She dropped down on the bed, looking at him.

"I got a call from the Trust Fund today."

"Oh?" He wasn't much interested in the Trust Fund. It was for Bonnie and Robie. Smythe, not Hendricks.

"You know what it is. It was set up by Brian's relatives, because Brian himself is so unreliable. Anyway, this man called me, and Robie gets a car for graduation."

Tom stared. "He does? When! What kind?"

"Tommy!" She looked as though she were about to cry. "Is that all you and Lionel think about? Cars?"

"Well . . . no . . ."

"But it's really so sad," she went on. "When I asked them if Brian was coming for Robie's graduation, no one seemed to know where he was."

That figured.

"Robie's counting on his father coming, and you'd think, too, that my dear ex-husband would want to see his daughter. Brian Smythe hasn't been much of a father."

"Right. Robie shouldn't count on Brian for anything."

"I know. But he does." She shook her head. "Robie's just kind of a lost soul."

Tom leaned against the wall and thought about him. It was really weird, about his stepbrother. Robie's dad had brought him into the family as a baby when he'd married Mom, and they'd been married—how long? Four years, five—long enough to have Bonnie, anyway—and then the bum had taken off. Robie had been left behind with his stepmother; his own mother was dead. It was almost as though he were a piece of unclaimed luggage. No wonder the guy had moods and said mean things.

"We are kind of an unusual family." He had sometimes tried to explain to his friends about the Hendricks-Smythe group, and the fact that he had a real brother, a half sister, and a stepbrother, but it all got so confusing he usually gave up. "We're *unusual*," he repeated.

"Right." His mother nodded. "Bonnie calls us a split-level family."

Tom laughed. His kid sis had quite a unique way of

putting things. The family called them Bonnie-isms.

He looked at his mother uneasily. "At least Robie gets good grades, and he can go to any college he wants to, I guess."

She nodded again, and then held up her hand as though to stop him from saying anything. Tom could hear slow steps coming down the hall.

"Hi." Robie peered in. "I turned on the oven and scrubbed some baking potatoes and put them in," he said. "I know Lion always wants baked potatoes when he's home."

"That's fine, Robie. Thank you."

Robie did sometimes try to be part of them, Tom thought. And he had helped to get all the old baby buggies and broken bottles out of the ravine.

He knew Robie was looking at him.

"I hear you're going racing tomorrow."

"That's right."

Tom jumped up and tried to touch the ceiling and missed. He knew his mother often wondered why they didn't ask Robie to go along with them, but the guy was absolutely no good around cars.

"Do you really expect to win anything with that heap of junk?" Robie asked.

Junk! Tom stopped jumping around and stared at him.

"Purple Haze. Purple *Craze* would be more like it. Do you call that a car?" Robie said.

"Car! It's a C Modified Production, is all. Listen, you—"

"Boys, stop that right now."

Tom could tell from his mother's tone of voice that she was getting irritated.

There was a thundering chug and blast from the garage, followed by a faint ping.

"What was that?" She jumped up, hands to her ears.

"It's just Lion, firing the Haze," Tom explained. "And that other little sound—well, I guess a cup popped out of the cupboard."

She got up wearily and looked around her. "Peace and quiet," she groaned. "Now. I would like you, Tom, to please tell Lion not to start his car up again until I have my shower and lie down for just fifteen minutes. And then find Bonnie and have her unload the dishwasher and set the table; it's her turn. Robie, there's a burned-out bulb in the hall; I'd appreciate it if you'd replace it."

Robie turned and then looked back.

"But about my graduation—"

"You heard the boss-lady. Come on." Tom could tell his mother had had enough of Robie's sadness, his own jumping around, and the Haze. "Relax for a while, Mom; I'll see that it's kept quiet around here."

"Thanks again for starting dinner," she called to Robie, as they went out.

Tom closed the door softly.

"She's kind of tired from her job," he told Robie. To himself he was thinking; *she didn't say we couldn't race.* She was keeping her promise.

They began working on the Haze right after dinner. Lion was anxious to check everything out and was muttering about linkage, talking even faster than usual. Tom was always surprised to find how much there was to do. Their mother and Bonnie had gone off and so they had the place almost to themselves.

Tom would fire the car while Lion looked to see what was going on. Before they knew it, it was eight thirty.

"Hadn't I better get in your jeep and go rent the tow bar?" Tom asked.

"I was hoping to get the loan of a truck," Lion said. "I'd rather load it up."

Tom didn't say anything. Lion had made two phone calls to people they knew who had trucks, but no one had been home.

"I've got five bucks, Lion. I was paid for some yard work yesterday. That's enough for the tow bar, and Mom said we could use the Chevy to tow it with."

Lion hesitated. "But she's not keen on the idea."

Tom nodded. She wasn't keen on any part of it.

"I know what I'm going to do," Lion said. "We leave so early that we surely wouldn't disturb anybody on this street, and if we go straight out Fortieth to Red Bud we'll be in the country . . . I wonder if it wouldn't be okay to drive it."

Tom looked at him in amazement. You couldn't drive a drag car on the streets! What was the matter with Lion, anyway! He'd been away from racing too long. That was what came of going off to college and cluttering your mind up with things like English and History.

"Lion—" he started. Then he paused. "It's illegal to drive a C Modified Production through the city."

"I know it's illegal. We'd have to get permission from the police."

Tom was sure this wouldn't work, but he hated to say so.

"Well, we could ask."

They went inside the house. Robie was sitting at

the kitchen table, college catalogues strewn around him.

"Still undecided about where you'll go?" Lion asked.

"Still undecided." Robie looked up. "What are you guys talking about? What goes on?"

"Not much, Step," Lion said.

They shook off their shoes and went on through the house to use the telephone extension in the hall. Tom waited while Lion dialed.

"Sir?" he heard Lion say, very politely. "I was wondering—" and he explained, still very politely, how he and his brother were going racing and they were trying to avoid the expense of a tow bar, and if they were very careful, could they, please, have permission to drive their racing car out of the city. "We hit Red Bud very soon and get out of the traffic; nothing but farms, out that way . . ."

The next thing Tom knew, there was Lion falling on the floor laughing.

"What did he say?" Tom asked. He couldn't stand it. Lion was rolling and choking with laughter.

"He said . . ." Lion gasped. "He said, 'Boy, you run that C Modified Production down Red Bud and the cows won't give milk for a week.'"

Tom had to laugh too.

Then he jumped over Lion and went for the tow bar.

As he ran through the kitchen Robie looked at him inquiringly, and Tom thought that he really should have stopped and told him what they'd been laughing about, but there just wasn't time. The Rent-A-Tool place closed at nine; he had to get the tow bar.

Chapter Two_____

"Youn-ger!"

Tom stirred as Lion shook him. It couldn't be six o'clock and time to go; it just couldn't be!

He rolled out.

The two dressed quietly, because Saturday morning was the only time their mother could sleep late, and then went on out to the kitchen.

The light was on.

"Be careful, you'll step on Viola Bloomer." Bonnie was standing in front of the refrigerator in her bathrobe.

Tom dodged the slinking striped shadow.

"I've never heard of a cat with two names before," he said.

"Viola Bloomer," Bonnie told him, "is a very unusual cat. Here." She pointed to a sack on the table. "I made sandwiches for you, and there's a thermos of juice."

Lion picked her up and threw her in the air and caught her.

"You are a good Bon Bon."

Tom would have liked a sandwich right then, but he remembered that they always stopped for something at the "Wagon Wheel" on the way to Alvad. He picked up the sack and thermos as they went by the table.

"When I get my own rig I'll name it after you, Bonnie."

"Great!" she said.

Lion was already in the garage. Tom shut the door carefully behind him as he went out, and to his surprise Robie's voice came from his room: "Good luck, you guys. And be careful."

"Thanks," Tom said. "See you later."

Everything was quiet along their street. Lion drove cautiously down it, the Haze bumping along behind, and Tom worried about the tires until he remembered that they'd be changing tires once they got to the track. The racing slicks were right behind them in the back seat of the Chevy.

He was always surprised to see how much was going on around town before seven in the morning; people waiting for buses on Fortieth, men in tin hats jammed into cars heading for the oil fields; trucks. When they got to Red Bud, Lion cornered very carefully and they were headed for the track. It wasn't necessary to turn again; they were all set. This was country. There were nothing but green fields and big trees and a few farmhouses. It was pretty out that way, Tom thought; just like a picture.

They rattled over an old bridge that looked as

though it had been built from a construction set, and, a little later, went by a pond. A mist was rising from the fields and Lion flipped on the radio, and there was Glen Campbell singing one of his great songs.

Tom was beginning to feel really hungry when they saw the low frame building with the red roof. Lion slowed up and pulled in beside a truck.

"Time for coffee and doughnuts."

It felt good to get out and stretch.

We must be about the youngest people in here, Tom thought, as they sat down at the counter. He looked rather uneasily at the leathery-faced men in faded work clothes sitting next to them, headed for a day pounding nails or hauling gravel, probably. *Do they think we're rich kids? We aren't.*

They had their coffee and doughnuts and got up to leave. One of the men called to them as they went by.

"You going racing?" he asked.

"Yes, sir," said Lion.

"I always kind of wanted to race."

Tom could feel eyes turn on them like searchlights. He wanted to stop and explain that Lion had earned their car, earned it pumping gas and doing yard work, but he didn't.

"Hope you win!" the same man said as they left, and Lion thanked him.

They got in the Chevy and started off again. Before they'd gone more than ten miles they began to see other racers headed for Alvad; Modified Cars, Stock Cars, and Gassers. Tom spotted a license plate from Kansas, which surprised him.

"Everyone wants experience," Lion said. "Just as we do. We're going to be all ready for the big one next month."

"You don't mean the big one at Western, here at home?"

"No, no. We're not ready for that. But we'll be ready for the points meet at Ringo."

Tom nodded, wondering if he would ever run the Haze himself. He never had.

It was getting warmer; it was going to be a hot, still day. That was just the kind of day Tom liked. He reached behind him and got his hat with the burned peacock feather. It was time to put on his racing hat.

"Remember when I got this?" he said, shaking the feather at Lion.

"Yeah. But get that thing out of my face." Lion was sitting up very straight now, and staring right ahead of him. "We're almost there. Man, I hope the officials won't disqualify me because of some stupid rule." He shook back his mop of hair and sighed.

"It'll be all right," Tom said.

"Do you 'feel' that it will be?" Lion laughed.

"Yeah. I feel it."

Lion thought he had a secret way of sensing things, and Tom himself sometimes believed that he did. He'd never made a team and couldn't even get his weight up, but he "felt" things.

Lion was sitting up straighter and straighter.

"All I hope is that I can pass requirements."

Tom nodded. He would have to be weighed in, and have everything checked for safety. They checked absolutely everything at a N.H.R.A. track.

"It'll be okay."

There was that sound; a buzzing, banging, snarling sound—the track. They couldn't see it yet, but they could hear it. A stock car painted red and white passed them; "Boss paint job," Lion muttered; an orange car was up ahead, and as Tom tried to figure out what kind it was, a green car, the color of a fruit drop, turned out from a side road.

They were there.

Tom tasted dust, and smelled scorched rubber from someone smoking his wheels. They turned into the driveway behind the car from Kansas. It was painted maroon, Tom noticed; a cobweb paint job.

"That has class," he said.

Lion nodded. He was staring at the car. "Chrome Crager Mag Wheels," he muttered.

It made Tom feel a little sad. They couldn't afford Cragers.

"I guess I'll get out and look around. I'll be right close by."

"Okay, Younger."

Tom got out of the car.

"Hi, man!"

An enormous figure in sweat shirt and cut-offs came loping up through the dust. It was Buck Williams, his eyebrows as black as two smudges of grease. He was a senior at Hoover and on the ball team. Both Tom and Lion had known him since grade school.

"Williams!" yelled Lion. "No practice today, huh?"

"Not until this afternoon. So I had to come out and watch my good buddies race." He picked Tom up and threw him on top of a nearby car.

Tom stared around him; he was lying on the curve of a burnished black surface. Oh well. He shrugged and slid off.

Williams tossed him up again.

Tom lay on his back and stared at the sky. It seemed to him that all his life either Lion had been knocking him down or Buck Williams had been tossing him around. *With a brother like Lion and a friend like Williams, I should have no difficulties in later life. I'm bound to be ready for anything.*

The surface beneath him moved; hastily, he slid off to the ground again. The car he'd been on was an old hearse, he noticed. And the thing was modified! It was going to race! It even had a name, "The Last Word."

"Are you racing?" Lion was asking Williams.

"No," he said. "I'm just here to see the cars. You know I sold my car. I gave you the steering wheel, didn't I?"

"You sure did." Lion patted the steering wheel as he got out of the Haze. "It's the most boss thing this car's got." He turned to look at Tom. "Let's get the racing slicks on now, before we weigh in."

"Sure thing."

"I'll be back to help you in a minute," said Williams, loping off.

Lion nodded but, as they started changing the tires, Tom knew that it wouldn't make too much difference if Williams came back or not; it was he, Tom, who was the wrench. He always knew when Lion wanted a lug or a four-way almost before it was needed. It was good to have extra help, though. That reminded him.

"Mom's always wanted us to ask Robie to come along when we race," he said suddenly.

"Oh no," Lion groaned.

But Tom was thinking, for some reason, *maybe we should have asked him.*

"He wouldn't like it at a place like this. Remember, when we cleaned up the ravine, how he hated getting so messy?"

That was right.

They had just got the slicks on and checked when it was their turn to be inspected. Tom was concerned because there was daylight showing around the shifter; Lion, he knew, was worried because they didn't have tailpipes or mufflers. There just hadn't been the time or money to get around to everything.

He could hardly bear to watch. If they were put in D.G. it would be all right, and in any event they would be able to race in some classification, but they wanted C Modified Production.

He jumped from side to side, restlessly. A black car, an Anglia named "The Stoned Rolls," went by them, and a red car named "Miss Carriage," and a souped-up station wagon. *I'll jump once more for luck.* He jumped, pretending he was making a tip-in. When he came down the tech man was writing C.M.P. on the back window of the Haze in big white letters. They'd made it!

"Your weight's all right, safety features all right, but next time . . ."

Someone nearby was firing and Tom couldn't hear the rest of the sentence, but he was sure Lion was being told that next time he'd better have mufflers.

It didn't matter. They'd made it.

He helped Lion get the car over to the pit and settled in the gravel.

"You ought to be proud," he said. "A lot of guys have their fathers or someone to help them and you've done it alone. Remember when Williams raced? His mother hired a mechanic to help him!"

Lion nodded. "I had some good help when I was home over Easter vacation, though."

"But you did most of it. You're doing good."

He nodded again. "And this summer we're *really* going to get into it."

They were all set for the moment. Tom ate a sandwich and then sat down in the gravel and looked around. A girl was perched up on the top row of the bleachers; there was nothing so unusual about that, as there were generally a few of them around any track. But there was something strange about this girl who was sitting up on the top bleacher all by herself.

She reminded him of Robie. Then he thought how stupid that was, since Robie and this girl were entirely different kinds of people. Even from a distance he could tell that the girl was good-looking and the type who would stand out in a crowd. Robie wasn't. *I wonder why she's alone.*

"Back in a minute, Lion," he said, and got up and went over to the stands. As he walked up toward her he realized that she was even better-looking than he had thought at first. He liked her long, dark hair and her big eyes.

"Hi," he said, and sat down just below her.

"Hi." She looked at him and then looked away. "I was just driving by on my way to the lake and this looked kind of interesting." She spoke as though she were explaining why she was there. "I get so bored," she said. "There's never anything to do." Then, before Tom could say anything, she asked, "Why do they drive such a short distance? And don't they go around curves?"

"You're thinking of round-and-round," Tom said. "Drag racing uses a quarter-mile track, and it's straight racing."

She nodded. "I know nothing about it."

Well, at least she wasn't one of those people who pretended to know something and didn't.

"First you race against time," he explained. "You don't race another car until elimination. Do you see that thing down there that looks like a fancy stop sign?" He pointed out the "Christmas Tree" to her, and she nodded. "You go by those lights."

She nodded again, and Tom wanted to ask her if she knew someone who was racing, but just as he opened his mouth, someone made a pass and the noise was deafening.

He stood up. He'd better get back, anyway. He noticed that the girl was wearing a sleeveless, ruffly little top of some kind; she was really going to get burned. He'd taken Bonnie swimming once and let her get burned and still felt guilty about it. A hat would help.

"Here." He took off his hat and handed it to her. "Wear it, please, or you'll get fried to a crisp," he said.

"Oh . . . thank you . . ."

"But take care of it. That hat has a history." He

turned and went back to the pit. Lion was sitting there having a cup of Bonnie's juice.

"How're we doing?"

"Great. Fire it for me, will you, while I watch? Then I'm going to take a plug-reading and we're all set."

Tom didn't even think of the girl again. Lion was soon ready to make his first pass. He watched him jerk his way up to the line for a time trial, thinking that it must be hard to hold down a C Modified. Lion was strapped in and had his helmet on. He was leaning forward, just a little; he always reminded Tom, at a time like this, of how he'd looked on the football field when he'd played end. The staging lights came on; the amber lights flashed—the green— off he went. He was shifting fast but not jerkily; you had to do it just right, Tom was thinking, because there were no handy buttons in a racing car. *There he goes; burning down the track and going good.*

He'd do even better later.

The driver of the fancy maroon car was talking to someone about Lion, using a very superior tone of voice.

"Not bad, but he won't make finals."

Ha!

It made Tom so mad he walked over to the bleachers and sat down. There was no point in getting hot and taking a poke at the guy. If you got into a fight at a track, you were invited to leave.

Was the girl still there? He turned and started to walk up the bleachers when he heard what had to be the Haze firing again, and it was. He swung around and looked down. There was Lion going up toward the black asphalt track in their car, and the maroon car, with the name "Blood" on it in gold letters, was fired and ready. As he watched, Lion gestured to the other driver and pointed down the track, and the driver nodded. Lion had decided to take him on. You were allowed to race another person in the trials if you wanted to and got permission, Tom remembered. It was sort of an unofficial race. *Lion must have heard that cat boast.* Tom jumped off the bleachers, staring.

They had started. Lion knew the lights better than the other driver and had "gate-jobbed" him, pulling out ahead of the maroon car. Then the Blood caught up with the Haze; they were side by side for a hair; then Haze pulled ahead. Lion had won! Tom jumped up and down, screaming. It was so great that Lion could outrun that dude, with his Chrome Crager Mag Wheels and cobweb paint job. Lion stopped and stepped out, very cool and collected, and Williams came running up, yelling; he had seen it too.

Tom ran toward them. "Great!" he said. "Great!"

"You'll take Street Elimination. You'll take it, man."

There was a ripping smear of sound.

Lion held up his hand. "Something's happening."

"So?" Tom asked. After all, something was always happening at a drag race. He looked in the direction Lion was pointing. The black Anglia had been doing a trial run and was out of control. Tom froze. He'd never seen a guy crash and burn; he didn't want to see it. He'd never even seen anyone do rail time. It had been bad enough that day at Western Speedway when the driver's clothes had caught on fire, but at least, there, the tech men had doused him in time. Lion and Williams were running toward the accident and Tom felt himself being pulled with them. He blinked his eyes against the smoke.

"They got him out," Lion said.

"I was about *lost*," Tom heard a voice yell.

Tom backed up and dropped down on the hood of a Volkswagen, and he had a sour taste from the doughnut he'd eaten earlier. It had been a close call. In front of him Lion and Williams were groaning and shaking their heads. There would be one less car racing that day.

Did that scare Lion as much as it did me? His brother sometimes got scared too; Tom could feel that he did. But he didn't dare ask Lion if the incident had frightened him. Lion would drop-kick him into the next state if he asked that.

Williams and Lion were now walking back to the pit. Tom followed. The real races were starting; if Lion had been at all shook, Tom realized, he gave no sign of it.

He watched, teeth clenched, as Lion won his way handily to the finals. Then he had to race a man who looked at least thirty, very blond and red-faced, with practically black hands. The red-faced man was driving a blue '57 Chevy. It wasn't as fancy as some of the others, and it didn't have a name, but Tom had a feeling that the owner of the blue Chevy knew what he was doing.

Lion may lose.

He winced, brushing the thought aside.

Lion started out well but then something went wrong. Tom held his breath; he had missed fourth gear, and over-tacked to do the bad side of ten grand. *Oh, no.* The Haze limped to the finish line, sounding sick. Lion had lost. He'd been just a little up-tight, perhaps. As he went back down the return road he looked at Tom and made a face and shook his head.

Tom groaned. Perhaps it had been too much to expect, that Lion would win. He'd been away from racing for almost a year while he was at Southern A. and M., and he hadn't really been at it as long as some of the others.

Williams was swearing and sputtering beside him.

"Now look, don't act as though it's such a big deal," Tom told him. "At least, he wasn't beat by someone like that stuck-up cat from Kansas."

"Okay. Okay." Williams nodded.

Lion didn't really seem too disappointed as he walked toward them; just asked if there was any cold juice left in the thermos.

"There sure is," Tom said. He and Williams had eaten the sandwiches, but they'd saved the rest of the juice for Lion.

"There'll be another time," Williams said.

Lion nodded. "That's the thing about racing. There's always another time."

"You did good, man," Williams said. He had his hand on Lion's shoulder. "I'll help you load up, and then I've got to split for practice."

It didn't take long to get ready to leave.

"It was worth it, wasn't it?" Tom asked, a little anxiously. Lion looked tired.

"Worth it? Of course it was worth it."

They got in the Chevy and started for home.

Williams passed them in his parents' station

wagon. His face was screwed up into a sneer. "See you at the finish line!" he shouted.

They were still laughing as they went down Red Bud. Tom thought, suddenly, about the driver who had done rail time. No one had mentioned him. No one had wanted to think of the man who had yelled, "I was about lost."

Chapter Three

TOM DOZED ON the way back, and woke up with a start just as they were going over the old bridge on Red Bud. He hadn't meant to go to sleep. One of the things he was supposed to do on these trips was to keep talking to Lion so that he would stay awake.

"Sorry, Lion—"

"S'all right."

"Did you do any damage to the Haze?" he asked.

"Not too bad. Bent two push rods."

It could have been worse.

Lion sighed. "But now I'll have to stay home and wrench, and I was counting on going to Western tomorrow to see the Fuelers." He sighed again. "I was going to go and take you."

"Western Speedway? You have the tickets, and everything?"

"Right."

"Someday we'll race at Western." Tom shook his

head. The thought was dizzying. "We'll run and win."

"Of course. But we're not ready for it yet. . . . We may be, after the Points Meet at Ringo," Lion said.

"Are you sure you can't go, tomorrow? If you have the tickets and everything . . ."

"No way." Lion shook his head, his bushy hair flopping. "I'll just have to stay home and wrench. And I've got to book a little, too . . . how're you doing at school? Okay?"

Tom was anxious to change the subject. "I guess," he said.

"Tell you what, Younger. You take the tickets and go to Western tomorrow, and I'll lurk around here. Ask Williams, or somebody. Take one of your friends."

"You're sure you can't go?" It didn't seem right to Tom. "They're going to have all those Fuelers and Funny Cars . . . everything!"

"No way, no way. I've got to lurk."

"Well, I'll sure go. Thanks."

They were on their street, and there was the house. They turned up the driveway and stopped in the circular area past the garage.

Robie came rushing out.

"How'd it go?"

"Great," said Tom. "Lion got to the finals, which is more than most of them did."

"I'm sure glad you're back, and all. I've been thinking about you."

He had been worried. The thought came to Tom as a shock. Robie wasn't really such a bad guy, except for his moods.

"Say, would you like to go to the races at Western with me tomorrow?"

"Western?"

That was typical of Robie, Tom thought. There probably wasn't another guy in Hoover (or girl, either) who didn't know about Western Speedway, just outside the city; it was famous. They even had the World Finals there.

"Yep. Western Speedway. It's a big meet. Lion has tickets, but he can't go."

"Why . . . I guess I'd like to go to it with you. Sure. Thanks; thanks a lot."

They went through the garage and on into the kitchen. Tom could smell chicken, and there was a pecan pie on the counter, and something simmering on the stove—either okra or greens. He lifted up the lid of the pot. Greens!

"Wash your hands. Why do you suppose I had those faucets put in the garage?"

He jumped. "Okay. Okay, Mom."

"I'm glad to see you're back, Tom."

"Are those mustard greens?"

"No. Turnip, poke, and beet, cooked together. I got them from my sister last night."

Heaven, thought Tom.

Bonnie rushed into the kitchen. "Tom, some girl named Valerie called you. She called twice! Who's Valerie? Where does she live? Does she go to Hoover? Are you going steady?"

"I don't know any Valerie," Tom said.

"She said she had a hat that belonged to you." Bonnie was looking at him intently. "She wants you to come right over and have a swim in her pool and get your hat."

His hat. He had completely forgotten about his racing hat. *That girl who was all alone. I gave her my hat.*

Puzzled, he went to the garage to wash his hands and then went back into the kitchen.

"How long before dinner, Mom?"

"About an hour." His mother was also looking at him intently; she wanted to know who Valerie was, too. "I'm waiting on the greens."

"I'd better go get my hat." He'd hate to lose that hat, because of the feather.

Tom managed to beat Lion to the shower but was careful not to take all the hot water, because in spite of the fact that Lion had been very nice about wanting him to go to Western, he knew that if he took all the hot water there would be trouble. He used cleanser and a nail brush, trying to get the grease off his hands. So this Valerie had a pool and wanted him to come over and swim in it. Well, he'd gone swimming in people's pools before; Buck Williams had a pool. They always wore cut-offs there, and cut-offs would have to do now; he hadn't owned a pair of trunks in years.

He took Lion's jeep, hoping it would get him there; Lion used it only to get home from college with, as it was stripped down and temperamental. He had the girl's address, written in Bonnie's round, neat writing. Valerie's home must not be very far from his. He hoped that she didn't live in some great big house like the Williams pad. It was a little strange, he thought, turning off their street onto Fortieth, that a no-account country lane (which was what their street was) had been caught up in the growth of the city so that it was in the suburbs. Their street was weird. Because there had once been the dump in the ravine, people still threw beer cans all over the place.

Tom made two turns and then paused beside a large stone house on the hill. *Wow.* He turned up the flower-bordered driveway. The people who lived here, he was sure, had no trouble with people dumping trash in their yard. He was glad he'd worn a shirt over his cut-offs.

A girl in a bikini was waiting for him by the side of the house in a diamond-shaped parking area; as he drove up, she waved. He parked, stopped the jeep, and got out.

"Hi!" she said, coming up to him. "Neat car!"

"This?" He glanced toward it. "At least, nothing fell out of it, this trip. It's my brother's; when he first got it I could always tell where he'd been, because things fell out of it wherever he went."

"Oh no!" She threw back her head and laughed. "Well. I'm Valerie Gates. And you're Tom Hendricks."

"Right. How'd you know my name?"

"It was written inside the hat. Your name and your phone number."

"Oh." Tom hoped that she didn't notice him swallow. There were several other things written there, too.

"Here." She handed him the hat with the burned feather. He took it, but what he was noticing was her figure.

"Thank you for loaning it to me." She smiled.

He had been hoping, for some reason, that she would have braces on, or messed-up teeth. She didn't. There was nothing at all wrong with her teeth.

"Without your hat I certainly would have gotten a sunburn. I have this pale skin. I have a terrible time getting a decent tan."

"Me too."

Valerie's skin was certainly white. On her, it looked good.

"I am so mad," she said. "My stepmother says the pool is filthy—they're coming to vacuum it Monday—and she doesn't think we should use it." She frowned. "She's so cross today it's pitiful. Her baby's been fussing and I know that's hard on her, but she takes it out on me."

Stepmother. Her baby. Not "my brother or sister," but her baby. So Valerie was split level, too.

She looked up at him. "That's quite a hat you have there, Tom."

He nodded and threw it into the jeep.

"You said that it had a history . . ."

"Oh!" He laughed. "A guy at Western Speedway was wearing a headband of feathers over his helmet when his Fueler caught fire . . ."

"Fueler?"

"It's a kind of racing car."

She seemed smart, and yet she didn't even know what a Fueler was.

"Go on, Tom."

"Well, his feathers caught fire. The car was on fire, as he went over the finish line. The officials went right out and doused it; he was okay. But I was in the crowd, and I managed to get one of the feathers, and stuck it in this old garden hat of my mom's."

It seemed rather silly as he described it, but Valerie had lit up like a pin ball machine.

"I think that's fabulous!"

Why would she think that was fabulous, Tom wondered. He had been looking around him a little as he spoke, and it was this house, this yard, that was fabulous. He had seen a lot of good-looking houses all around Hoover High and he lived in a nice house, but this place wasn't a house. It was a mansion.

"We don't have to just stand here," she said quickly. "Would you like to look around?"

"Yes." Tom nodded.

She started off and he followed her, a little uncertain of what to say.

"Do you go to Hoover?" he asked finally.

She shook her head.

"I go to Field Academy."

That figured. She was the private-school type. Robie, he remembered, had once gone to Field.

"Here's the pool."

He stared. The pool itself was a big rectangle, like most pools, but behind it was a little stream with a waterfall, and there was a jungle-like growth of trees and shrubs and flowers, and he could see the white flash of a statue in the sun.

He whistled.

"You're certainly lucky to live here."

"I know." Valerie nodded. Why did she seem sad, as she said it?

"I do like our sun deck," she said, suddenly. "I like the orange umbrellas. They aren't so old. Everything else is so old."

At the deep end of the pool was a stairway leading up to the roof above their garage. It looked bare, to Tom, in spite of all the sunchairs and bright umbrellas, but he didn't say so. Class, he thought. This all has class.

She went over to the stair and started up.

"Isn't school a drag?" she asked him.

Now they were on the same wave length.

"It is," he groaned. "But I thought you 'Fielders' were enthusiastic about school."

"Nah." She sighed. "Oh, I do pretty well, and I have a good memory and can get stuff when I want to." She turned and looked at him as they reached the sun deck. "But I hate it."

Tom nodded and stared down at the pool below them.

"It's the same thing day after day. People sitting around wondering about who they are really, or telling you how great they think a *A Separate Peace* is."

Tom felt confused. The people he knew did not sit around wondering who they were. And what was "A Separate Peace"? A rock group, probably.

"I suppose you like *A Separate Peace*," she groaned.

"Well, let's face it," he said. "They'll never be as good as 'The Jackson Five.' "

Valerie had started to say something but stopped; her face smoothed into surprise and then he heard her laugh.

"What—" he asked.

"I—I'm sorry," she said. She was choking. "*A Separate Peace* is a book."

All he wanted to do was to get out of there quick—disappear, hide.

"That will be all, Miss Gates."

He bowed, deeply. Then he turned and, making sure he would clear the pool's edge if he jumped, sprang into the air, did a jackknife, and even remembered to keep his head down so that he would hit the water cleanly. The pool felt cold and good. He surfaced near the edge, climbed out without bothering to find a foothold, ran down to the jeep, jumped in and took off for home.

Robie heard him and came down the steps toward him, blinking. "Wow! The Monster from the Deep!"

"Just don't yell at me," Tom snarled. "I can't stand people yelling at me."

"Okay, but come on up here and I'll lend you a shirt; Mom'll wonder what happened."

He was right. Tom hurried up to Robie's big, tidy room and by the time his mother had started looking for them he was in a clean shirt of Robie's and had his hair slicked back with a towel.

"What's going on?" she asked.

"Not a thing," said Robie. "We were just discussing the tragedy of Viet Nam and World Conditions."

"I'll bet. Well, dinner's ready; come on."

Tom had hoped that he could spend the evening helping Lion work on Haze, but his mother had other plans.

"It's your turn to put the things in the dishwasher. And I notice that you never did finish mowing that strip of grass by the ravine."

He groaned. She was right. The old man in the tumbledown house next to them had given him five dollars to do his yard and to trim, and he'd gone over there because he'd needed the money.

"Robie'll do it," he said.

"Robie will not do it. It's your turn. Besides, he has a date with Mary."

Robie always had a date with this Mary on Saturday nights, Tom knew. *I should be glad he has a chick.* He didn't seem to have any friends, but at least he had a chick.

"If I only could be sure Brian would be here for his graduation!"

Tom looked at his mother. She was standing beneath the kitchen light, and the frown lines in .her face showed. She really had a lot on her mind.

"He'll probably show. Don't worry about it. Look, isn't this your bowling night?"

"Well, yes, they're coming by for me in a minute. But this place is such a mess . . ." She looked around her. "You'll have to scrub out the roaster, and those two foil-covered pans go into the freezer . . . Oh, and Tom." She sighed. "Some man in a pickup dumped a whole load of junk at the end of the street . . ."

"I'll take care of things, Mom. You go ahead. And I'll clean up the junk, too." She needed her bowling.

"Okay." She went off to change her clothes, already looking more relaxed.

"I'll do the pots and pans if you do the dishes." Bonnie came into the kitchen with Viola Bloomer.

"Fine, Bonnie-Belle."

He got everything done, with Bonnie's help. By this time his neck was beginning to sting like fire. He had really got a burn, this time.

"Have you got anythng to put on a sunburn, Bon Bon?"

She shook her head.

"Look up in Robie's loft. There might be some in his bathroom; he always has a lot of stuff like that."

It was true that Robie always had "stuff," but Tom felt a little doubtful about going up into the loft while Robie was out. He hesitated, and then went up the three steps to the big room above the garage.

It was as neat as a store window. Robie's desk was clear except for a big stack of envelopes, and above it

was the bulletin board with all the acceptance letters
Robie had received from colleges. The bulletin
board, Tom noticed, was labeled "My Future" in big
black letters. Something about the label made Tom
uneasy.

He found some lotion in the bathroom and put it
on his neck. Below him, he could hear the boom of
voices; Williams and some others had come over to
help Lion work on his car. Tom hurriedly went on down
and rolled out the mower. If he got through with the
yard work early enough he might be able to wrench
along with the rest of them.

The strip of lawn wasn't very big but the ground was
uneven, and it seemed to Tom that doing that one little
patch and making it look right was taking him hours.
His neck still stung; he ached all over. It had been a
long day. He finished, finally, and then got some bags
and went along the street picking up cans.

"Are you still at it? I'll help!"

Bonnie, wearing one of his old T-shirts that swung
below her knees, ran toward him.

"Oh, this is pretty rank, Bonnie. You'll cut your
hands."

"I've got on Mom's gardening gloves."

"Good girl!"

The worst of the mess was at the end of the street
where the guy in the pickup had unloaded his
goodies. Tom almost wished that his little half sister
wasn't there, because he would have enjoyed ripping
out with some expressions that he didn't like to use in
front of Bonnie. They had just finished when a gleaming car stopped at the entrance to the street and a
woman opened the door and threw out some Kleenex

tissues and all the cigarette butts from her ashtray.

"Lady, please!" Tom yelled.

She glared at him.

"Don't you loudmouth me, young man."

"But you're dumping your junk . . ."

"I thought this was a dump, along here!"

Bonnie ran toward the car.

"We live here!" she said. "It's not a dump! We cleaned it all up, and we're trying to keep it clean!"

"Sorry, hon," the woman said, and the car took off.

Bonnie turned to Tom. Tears were running down her face.

"That lady thinks we're her garbage pail," she said.

"Oh, Bonnie . . ." He would have hugged her, but he was too smelly and dirty. "Bon Bon, you can't let things like that bother you."

But of course it bothered her, he thought. It would have bothered anybody.

"Hey," he said. "Isn't that your cat?"

Ordinarily Tom was not happy to see the hunched shape of Viola Bloomer, but maybe the cat would take Bonnie's mind off the lady in the car.

"Yes! Viola Bloomer, where have you been?" She grabbed her and ran toward the house.

That Bonnie. She is something. Tom could not imagine why his stepfather hadn't come back to see her more often; Brian Smythe was a no-good. He ought to be proud that he had a daughter like Bonnie. For that matter, he ought to be proud to have a son like Robie.

Tom finished filling the sack and dragged it down the street to the place where the city truck would pick it up. There was another one he'd left; might as well finish up. He could hear talk and laughter from the garage. Lion and Williams and some others were having a good time working on the Haze, while he slaved. Oh well.

It was dark, by now. He had a hard time finding the other sack they had filled, and when he did find it, it had fallen over and spilled and he had to refill it.

"Watch it, man!"

Williams roared past him in a car; two others were with him. So they were all through wrenching. He'd missed it.

Wearily, he dragged the sack down the dark street. The whole evening had certainly been a down. He paused by the tumbledown shack to listen to the music coming from the blue glare near an open window. The only other house on their street was certainly a wreck, but at least they had a television set. The music cut off suddenly and the news came on:

". . . Seventeen-year-old youth drove his car down Linden Lane into River Road and rammed himself into the old viaduct on the bank of the Arkansas River . . ."

It was the second time that had happened that month. Tom listened, feeling faintly sick, for the boy's name. It was no one he knew. *Why would anyone want to kill himself?* Then he gave himself a little shake and went on toward his house.

Lion was still in the garage, still working. Tom could see his feet sticking out from under the car.

"I thought you were going to wrench tomorrow, Lion! And that was why you couldn't go out to Western . . ."

"I'll be wrenching tomorrow too. And booking."

The garage had that lonely look a place gets when a lot of people have left, Tom noticed, and Lion's radio, beside him on the floor, was playing music with that tinny, echo-like sound you hear in empty places. There were cans from a six-pack beside the radio.

"Did everybody cut out?"

"Everybody cut out."

That was what they did when it got late, and when they got tired, and when the beer was gone. They left.

"How's it going?" Tom asked.

"Got it fixed."

"Good." Tom had a hard time sounding enthusiastic. It was Lion's car, anyway. He'd never run it, probably never would run it.

"Got it fixed," Lion repeated. "Everything works. But now I'm trying to find out *why* it works."

"Great," Tom said, feeling the back of his neck.

"Would you fire it for me just once, Younger, while I look at something under the hood?"

"Sure. Wait; is Robie up there?"

"Not back yet. He took his chick to some cultural event."

Tom nodded. They were always going to some cultural event. He got in the car and fired it. Lion looked intently into the engine and then signaled that he should stop it; he stopped it.

"I'm bushed," Tom said, as he got out of the car. "I'm going to turn in. You should, too."

"I will in just a minute. Thanks."

Tom went inside. There was one piece of pecan pie left; he polished it off. If there was anything he loved, it was pecan pie. He began feeling better. *And I'll be going out to Western, tomorrow.* He went through the house and checked Bonnie's room; she was asleep, with Viola Bloomer stretched beside her. *I'm glad she has her stupid cat.* He stripped and showered. Even his sunburn didn't seem to hurt as much, now. A wavering tinkle of music still came from the garage. It was Lion's transistor; Lion was still out there in the garage trying to figure out why something worked. Tom smiled as he slid into bed. The music was dim and far away and sweet, and it was only a rinky-dink radio, but it sounded good. He was still listening to it as he dropped off to sleep.

 *Chapter Four*_____

Tom and Robie started out to Western Speedway fairly early, in, to Tom's relief, the Chevy. The jeep was too unpredictable.

"How did you say Mom and Bonnie were getting to church?" Robie asked, a little worried. Bonnie always wanted to go to church.

"Mom's sister's taking them."

Funny, that Robie would have worried about this, and he hadn't.

"Let me tell you about this play I went to last night." Robie was looking studiously at the road as he spoke.

Tom stirred, restlessly, beside him. There would be no way to stop him from talking about the cultural event he had gone to the night before with his chick.

"This was a modern interpretation of *Oedipus Rex*. You know, the Greek drama about the son and mother and father."

"I do not know," Tom said. After faking it with Val-

erie about that book, he was never going to try anything like that again. "How do you spell it?" He
asked, suddenly, and Robie spelled it out. Well, he
thought, that explains something. He had seen a stock
car once with the name "Oedipus *Wrecks*," and had
always wondered what the deal was.

Robie was going on and on about this play, but, to
Tom's relief, they were coming to a big motel called
King Arthur's Court (Ye Olde English Castle) with its
moats and towers and courtyard. Some of the racers
were loading up their cars.

"What are they?" Robie asked.

"Those are some of the racing cars."

"The racers stay *here?*"

"Right. They always do. I don't think they care much
about Ye Olde English atmosphere, but this motel
happens to be near the track."

"Quite a contrast in life styles," Robie murmured.

Robie, Tom thought wearily, could hardly give you
the time of day without making it sound like a page
from the Encyclopedia.

He slowed up. "Wouldn't you like some pancakes?
They have a place to eat, here."

Pancakes! The only thing he liked better than pancakes was Squaw Bread, and Squaw Bread was hard
to come by.

"I sure would!"

Robie had turned.

"Remember, Dad used to pick us all up after Sunday
School and church and take us somewhere for pancakes?"

Tom nodded, although his memories of his stepfather
were very dim. He never even thought of him as

"Dad," but as "Brian"—when he did think of him. He had no respect for Brian Smythe. How could you respect somebody who spent most of his time lying around drunk?

The pancakes were good, but Robie took his time with breakfast and Tom began to feel restless. He wanted to get out to the track early, before things started. He liked to see the racers unload.

As they stood in line at the cashier's, a woman in a hat was saying: "I had no idea they had earthquakes in this part of the country!"

"They don't, honey." The cashier smiled.

"I was in your East Tower and it rocked all night," the woman said. "I know you have tornadoes down here, but you have earthquakes, too!"

"It's the racers," the cashier said. "The place is full of racers, hon. They run up and down the halls playing tricks and hexing each other."

Robie waited patiently in line while the two women talked. If it had been Lion, Tom thought, he would have just plunked down the money and split. But Robie was not Lion.

The racers were loading up Funny Cars when the two boys came out into the courtyard.

"What are those!"

"Funny Cars."

"They don't look so funny, exactly . . ."

"I know," Tom said, thinking that it was certainly unusual for him to be explaining something to Robie. "And they aren't funny. They are just a certain kind of modified car. The first ones had the front and back wheels rather close together, and of course they do stand rather high, and somebody saw one and said, 'What a funny car!' and so they started calling them 'Funny Cars.' They're experimental," he said, "and it was an easier mouthful than Super-Experimental-Stock-Car."

"I remember." Robie nodded. "Lion explained to me once that a lot of new automotive developments are tried out at race tracks."

Tom nodded. "Lion knows all about it. He can really rap about how drag racing has improved cars by trying out different things on the track."

"That's very interesting."

"You haven't seen anything yet, man. Wait'll we get out to Western and you see a Fueler!"

"A Fueler?"

Robie was really impossible, Tom thought, in discouragement. He didn't even know what a Fueler was.

Apparently, though, his stepbrother had become curious, because he drove much faster the rest of the way. Tom even became a little alarmed.

"You're making pretty good elapsed time!"

"Yeah." Robie slowed down. "What is *that!*" he pointed.

"That's a Double-A Fueler."

He let Robie take it in; the long, low, stretched-out-looking body; the big, doughnut-shaped wheels at the end.

Robie was silent as they found a parking place.

"It looks like something out of science fiction! Will that thing run?"

"It'll run," Tom said. "It'll run about 225 miles an hour. Sometimes more."

"Impossible! And you told me once that they just go a quarter mile—how can they stop!"

"You'll see." He didn't want to tell him. He wanted Robie to see how they stopped them.

Western Speedway was already jammed, as they entered.

"It's sort of like the fair," Robie muttered.

Tom nodded.

It was like a fair. All kinds of people were there; big guys, little guys, couples, chicks; and no one was worrying about Viet Nam, or the college of their choice, or a job; no one seemed to be worrying about anything. An old man in a flowered shirt rushed at them eating a hamburger, and Tom, dodging him, nearly ran into a girl with long blond hair. Something about her reminded Tom of Valerie, although Valerie was dark and this girl was blond. *Valerie. I blew it with Valerie.*

"Tom, you have the tickets, but you didn't get a Pit Pass. Don't you want one?" Robie asked.

"Well, yes." He wanted one the worst way, but he didn't have enough to get two Pit Passes and cold drinks, later. You always got so thirsty at the track.

"I'll get them. What is the pit, anyway?"

"Well—" Tom pointed. "It isn't really a pit, like a big hole. Look over there where the racers are working on their cars. It's just a gravel place where they get the cars ready."

"It's where the action is?"

"It's where the action is." Robie was beginning to catch on.

As they got the passes and went toward the pit

Tom thought that this was one of the few times that
either he or Lion had asked Robie to go somewhere
with them, or do something with them. They had gone
to movies together when they were in grade school,
and down to the "Y" and to Little League, but in the
last few years they had left Robie out. That was bad.

As they reached the pit, Tom took a deep breath and
looked around, smiling. He liked the sound of men
working on cars, and the noise of an engine firing, and
the smell of fuel.

"These guys all help each other?" Robie asked,
surprised, staring at one man who was handing another a wheel.

"Sure. Racers, especially the ones who have Fuelers,
often give each other a hand. I've seen guys lend
other guys *engines.*"

Robie nodded, but hung back a little. He didn't
like grease and dirt, Tom knew.

"I can hardly wait until you hear a Fueler take off,"
he said. "It will blow your mind."

"Ha!" Robie grinned. "You forget that I have to live
above a monster called Purple Haze."

Tom laughed. It was good to hear Robie talking like
any other ordinary, goofing-off cat.

"There's quite an outfit, Youngie."

Tom turned to look at it. It was. The Fueler was
bronze with a black stripe, and the men working on it
wore bronze uniforms with a black stripe down the
pants leg, and beside them on the gravel was the
driver's gold-colored helmet.

"I want to see the name on that dude," Robie said.

He dropped back a little, and as Tom started to
follow he heard a voice that was somehow familiar.

"Sure dig these things! *Groovy*."

It was some guy trying to talk like a kid. It was
. . . *oh no, No.*

The voice sounded like Brian.

Robie's old man. My stepfather. Could Brian Smythe
really be here?

"Please don't touch that."

One of the racer's crew had turned to the speaker.

It would be just like Brian to bug one of the racers,
Tom thought, although even the stupid little junior-
high kids who came out here knew that you weren't
supposed to bother the racers or mess with their stuff.
Equipment and parts for Fuelers were expensive and
you didn't touch *anything.*

Brian was the type who would.

Tom stared at the man ahead of them, a fairly tall
individual with thick brown hair, just a little gray
now, in places; there were crumpled-up places around
his eyes, and he needed a shave. His shirt was dirty.
He looked so messy generally that Tom wasn't sure it
was Brian, because Brian had once been a rather
good-looking man and what his mother called a sharp
dresser. He had not seen his stepfather in two years.
When had it been that Brian had steamed into town
with a big doll for Bonnie (who had never cared for
dolls) and a catcher's mitt for Robie (who had never
really liked ball); two years ago, or three?

He glanced at the man's left hand. The index finger
was missing. It was Brian.

Tom stepped back, vaguely worried. Had Brian
come back to see his children? And if so, why hadn't
he showed around the house, or called them? He
hadn't. And he supposedly lived in California, now.

"Do you happen to know if Tommy Smothers is racing today?" Brian was asking the racer. "Or Benny Osborne?—The Wizard has got to be here—this is his territory!"

Tom never heard the racer's answer. *This explains it.* Brian had come from California for the races. It wasn't World Finals or anything, but it was a big race, and most of the men you read about in "National Dragster" were there. Brian was right here in town, the place where his kids lived, and he hadn't even bothered to get in touch with them.

Tom felt a prickle of perspiration all over him. In just a second, Robie would catch up with him. And then . . .

"Checked into King Arthur's Court on Friday," Brian was saying. "Where you speed demons are staying. What were you guys doing, last night, racing around the courtyard on your mini-bikes! Wild!"

"Couldn't say, sir." The voice was trying to be polite. "I was trying to get some sleep, myself; I don't have a bike."

Tom was trying to think. He had to stop Robie from running into his old man, stop him from finding out that the guy had been here for two days without even phoning him.

What to do.

He went after Robie and grabbed him and asked if he'd noticed the Funny Car called "Stardust." Robie had been wanting to see one up close. The Funny Cars were behind them, in the opposite direction. If he could get Robie to move he had it made. They wouldn't run into Brian. Much as Robie wanted to

see his dad, this wasn't the time. Besides, Tom was
sure that Brian was drunk. He talked in a strange,
lagging way, like a record being played at the wrong
speed.

"Well . . ." said Robie. "What's so special about this
'Stardust'?"

"Wait'll you see it," Tom said, pushing him. "These
cars are officially called Double-A Stock, now, and—"
He dragged him along.

The next time he looked for Brian, the figure in the
dirty shirt had disappeared in the crowd. *Safe for
now.*

The races had started and they went to the stands
and settled down to watch.

"That car!" Robie yelled. "It looks like they're opening it with a can opener!"

"That's another Funny Car. They have to get to the
engine that way."

Tom was rapidly forgetting about the barely missed
meeting with Brian.

When the Fuelers raced, Robie grabbed Tom and
shook him.

"You've got to tell me how they stop. You've got to."

"*Look*, man."

A Fueler was scorching toward the finish line. Then
its parachute opened, bright red.

"Outa *sight!*"

Tom laughed. Robie was really digging it.

It was late in the afternoon when they got back.
Lion was in the garage, and rushed out toward them.

"Hey!" He hit Tom the minute he got out of the car.

"A chick's been calling you all day!" He turned to Robie.

"How'd you like the drags, Step?"

"Very much. Very colorful. I can certainly understand why, with everything so sort of dehumanized and all, those races would have mass appeal."

There he goes, sounding like an Encyclopedia again, Tom thought disgustedly. Oh well. He'd had a good time while he was there, anyway.

"Tom!" Bonnie called. "You're wanted on the phone!"

He rushed through the house to the phone in the hall, and to his surprise heard Valerie's voice, rather breathy and little-girl sounding.

He hadn't blown it.

"Tom," she said, "I'd like to ask you to be my escort for Spring Cotillion. It's next Friday, at Southland Country Club. If you have no other plans for that evening, that is."

"Why—" *What is Spring Cotillion?* "I have no plans for that evening," he said. He seemed to be having some trouble breathing. "I'd like very much to be your escort for Spring Cotillion."

Chapter Five

Tom's FIRST CLASS that Monday was Auto Mechanics. He was glad, because Auto Mech was the only class he really liked, and with Mondays always such a drag it was great to have one good thing going. Auto Mech didn't seem like a class, anyway; you walked into a big, echoing room, with the familiar smells of grease and oil, and people walking around and yelling at each other. You didn't have to keep still in Auto Mech. Tom changed into the old clothes he kept there to work in.

"Youngie!" a voice called; he didn't even mind being called Youngie. "Hear Lion did pretty well up at Alvad!"

"Made Street Elimination," he called back. "Got beat, but we did all right."

"Good for him!"

And it *had* been good, he thought, jerking up his pants. He was finally putting on a little weight;

the pants were tight. It had been quite a weekend, the whole thing; going to Alvad, and then seeing the races on Sunday. Of course, there had also been that scary moment when Robie had almost run into his old man there in the pit, but he brushed that aside.

And on top of all that, Valerie Gates had called him. He must remember to find out about this Spring Cotillion thing. He could ask Williams, he decided. Big old Buck might know about it. He knew a lot of people who went to Field.

"Tom!" Mr. Pop was calling.

"Yes, sir," he said, and went over to him on the double.

The Auto Mech teacher's real name was Mr. Poplinger, but everyone called him Mr. Pop.

"Got a job here, Tom," he said. "You know, we sometimes work on one of the teachers' cars, if the problem's not too difficult."

Tom nodded.

"Of course, I realize that this isn't what you're used to, Tom," Mr. Pop went on, smoothing back his one lock of hair over his bald head. "Sorry we don't have a Fueler for you to work on. Or a Funny Car."

He knew perfectly well that Lion raced C Modified, Tom thought, trying to keep his face straight. Mr. Pop was all right.

"It's okay, sir."

"Fine. Now Tom, this is Mr. Ellers' car—"

All the good feeling went away. If there was anyone Tom could not stand, it was Mr. Ellers. Mr. Ellers taught Social Studies, and Social Studies was a drag.

"I'd like you to clean these spark plugs and re-gap them."

Tom almost groaned out loud. He knew that after he'd done the job (no problem) Mr. Pop would want him to retake the written test on this that he had flunked the week before. He had never been able to take written tests. It wasn't that school work was so difficult; he understood it well enough when it was discussed; it was the writing down of facts, any facts, that threw him.

He started in, wishing that he'd been asked to do some simple thing like clean the racks.

When he had finished, Mr. Pop checked everything over and told him that it was fine. They talked for a moment, and then the teacher said:

"Now, Tom, I want you to retake that test."

"Do I have to?" he asked. "I mean, the main thing is that Old Man Ellers—that *Mr.* Ellers' car will run better, now."

"The main thing is the work, certainly." He nodded. "But I have to mark you on a test. It's just a short one, Tom."

There was nothing for it but to sit down and take the test. Tom got the tight feeling he always got. He hated any kind of tests. He had something against them, he thought; or they had something against him. Words smudged as he put down them, and what had been clear and easy a moment before seemed a hopeless tangle. But, as he answered these questions, something unusual happened. "I know this stuff," he told himself. "And I know I know it." He felt accelerated and confident. The tight sensation began to lessen; he had one of his feelings. *I am passing this test.*

Tom passed the test. He stared, unbelievingly, at the paper. "B+." It was nothing for Lion or Robie to get a "B," and Bonnie never saw anything but an "A," but for Tom, getting a decent mark was a new experience. He was so startled that he was almost late for English, and he was a few minutes late for the following class, Social Studies, because he had run all the way back through the long halls to Auto Mech to ask Mr. Pop if he really had passed.

"Of course you passed," Mr. Pop said, his voice booming out from under the hood of a car. "I'd have given you an 'A' but I had to knock off a little for spelling. There's nothing wrong with your headbone, Tom."

That was news. He walked into Social Studies in a daze.

"Nice you could make it, Tom." Mr. Ellers had a rather prissy, precise little smile that he reserved for students who displeased him.

Stupid Diddle-Dee-Do-Gooder, I should have dropped an egg in his engine.

He slid into his seat.

Class started up again. Mr. Ellers was reading something out of a book called *The Lonely Crowd.* Even the name of the book sounded crazy to Tom. *How can you be a lonely in a crowd?* Suddenly there was an odd kind of silence in the room and Tom realized that Mr. Ellers was asking him a question. He had switched from the book to a newspaper article, and Tom sat there, tense, hoping that the teacher would say something more to clue him in.

"Do you think this editorial is right, Tom?" Mr. Ellers asked. "Do you think that people in a slum area are at fault for not doing more to help themselves?"

"No," he said, automatically. He was thinking about the night he and Bonnie had cleaned up the street and then the lady had dumped out her ashtray—"as though we were a garbage pail," Bonnie had said.

"Can you give us a reason?" asked Mr. Ellers.

"It may be very hard to help yourself if you live in a slum," he said, slowly trying to explain. "Maybe other people *like* slums. They *like* having a low-grade place to dump things in, and low-grade people to blame things on."

"What's that again?" Mr. Ellers looked puzzled.

A girl over against the wall said, "I think I know what Tom means," and pretty soon everybody was talking. Mr. Ellers looked surprised.

Tom himself was surprised.

At noon he usually found somebody to go to the Drive-In with, or to one of the pizza or taco places; there was also Perry's, where they had very good chicken-fried steak. Perry's was popular because it was right next to the Family Fun Center, in case you felt like shooting a few games of eight ball instead of going to Fourth Hour. But that day he didn't go to Perry's. He didn't want to be tempted by the idea of shooting pool. Also, he decided, if he split for home, he could save coins by grabbing something out of the refrigerator. Luckily he spotted his friend Motor-Mouth Murphy (so called because he had a talent for chatter when he was in the outfield). Motor-Mouth gave him a ride across the playing field on his cycle, and let him off right at the entrance of the street. Tom ran down the road and hurried up his driveway. He was looking forward to just sitting there quietly in the kitchen with a loaf of bread and a bottle of milk, thinking about all the things that had happened, and what was going to happen next; sorting it out. It was good to be by yourself once in a while to sort things out.

He went through the garage, giving Purple Haze a slap, and on through the back door.

Robie was sitting there at the kitchen table.

"Oh," Tom said, and looked at him. He *would* be here.

"Hi, Step," he said quickly. "Say, that was sure fun Sunday, wasn't it!"

"Yes, it was. I certainly did enjoy it."

But Tom had been too late with his cheerful words. Robie already had his I'm-afraid-I'm-going-to-get-kicked-in-the-teeth expression.

"I knew you'd dig those Fuelers."

"I've been coming home for lunch because I'm more or less expecting a call from my dad," Robie said quickly, as though explaining something. "Dad doesn't usually write, you know. He calls."

Tom couldn't look at him. The truth of the matter was that "Dad" didn't usually do much of anything, and of course at that moment the bum was right in town, at King Arthur's Court. Tom opened the refrigerator.

"Wash your hands," Robie said. "And what are you going to do with that loaf of bread?"

"I'm going to eat it," Tom said. "You're worse than Mom."

"Just trying to shape you up, Youngie."

Viola Bloomer sneered at the window, which meant that she wanted to be let in, and then the telephone rang.

"Peaceful around here." Tom sighed. He'd come home to sort things out, and his stepbrother and the cat were bugging him. And the phone was ringing.

"Let Viola Bloomer in," Robie said, as he rushed to the phone.

Tom was opening the door for the cat when he had a sudden thought. Robie might know about this Spring Cotillion.

"Oh, hi, Mary," Robie was saying.

He certainly didn't sound very excited about being called by his chick. Of course, he was expecting a call from his no-good old man.

"Yes, I'm getting this car. Want to come with me?"

He wasn't even excited about getting a car.

Robie hung up while Tom was on his third sandwich and came back to the table.

"I don't see how you can eat so much," he gasped. "You aren't human. And sit up. And stop slopping."

"I'm not slopping." But he sat up. He'd better mind his manners, if he was going to this elite party. "Say, do you know anything about Spring Cotillion?"

"Not much," Robie said. "It's a very nice party, I understand. The girls who are going to it are written up in the society page of the Sunday paper—as you'd know, if you ever read anything but car magazines."

Tom got up and managed to find the Sunday paper. Sure enough, there was Valerie's picture, all right, standing in a line with a bunch of other girls. They were all wearing long white dresses.

"You'll need to rent a tux if you're going," said Robie. "Look, I'll lend you some money for the weekend, if you're short." And before Tom could stop him he was pulling out a ten spot and giving it to him.

"Listen—"

"It's okay, *okay*."

He was very nice about things like that. When Bonnie was selling Camp Fire candy, he'd bought ten boxes, Tom remembered, and he didn't even like candy.

"It's not as bad as it might be. The girl's family furnishes the corsage, and there's a supper of some kind or an after-party so you don't have to worry about chow, and so the tab's not as high as you'd think."

Tom thanked him and took off.

That was what he wanted to know.

The afternoon dragged. Finally, it was three thirty, and Tom hurried out to find Williams. He was the one who could tell more about the party.

The baseball team was already at practice. They were big shots, the lordly Sixth Hour guys; they had gym the last thing, and then went right on after school into practice. Tom walked over to the diamond, and there was Williams, catching flies. Most of the team were taking a break, but a few of the eager beavers were working straight through. He stood there for a minute, watching. To see Williams catch a fly was something. He was out there all alone in the big green field, and, because he was Williams, was chewing a wad of bubble gum bigger than anybody else's wad. When the ball was hit he didn't even seem to brace himself, just stood there, all set, and blew his first bubble. Then he moved a little closer in and blew his second bubble. He caught the ball on the third bubble. To Tom, it was a beautiful thing to watch.

He stood there for a moment remembering what it had been like to play ball himself, almost feeling the thud of the ball in his mitt, hearing the crack of the bat. He'd played right up until last year. Baseball had been his one chance; he was too light for football, and not quite coordinated enough for track. The trouble was that Hoover was so big. You had to be really good, to make a team and to be a Sixth Hour guy. He hadn't made it. He hadn't done much of anything, when you got right down to it; he couldn't even get a decent tan. Lion's younger brother—that's all he was.

"Youngie?"

Old Buck Williams had seen him standing there and had come loping over to see what he wanted. He hadn't dared interrupt him at practice to ask him stupid questions about a party, but Williams had sensed that he wanted to talk. They were pretty good friends.

"Something on your mind, man?"

Tom ducked as Williams swung at him.

"Right. Have you ever been to one of those Spring Cotillion things?"

Williams shook his head.

"I know what it is, though. My sis went to it. It's this fancy party for girls. *And* their parents."

"Oh." Well, he'd known it was fancy.

"Tom Tom! Youngie-Bungie! Tom Tom *Tom!*"

There was Motor-Mouth, jabbering away as usual. Entire ball games had been won by Motor-Mouth, who made so much racket nobody could keep his mind on what was happening. Someone pushed Tom from behind; it was Delbert Kane, another ball player, towering over Tom in his green sweatshirt.

"Hi, Kane," Tom said, remembering that Kane hated

being called "Delbert." You had to be careful not to call him the "Jolly Green Giant," too; he'd made that mistake, once, and felt the bruises for a week.

"Spring Cotillion?" Kane asked. He had apparently heard part of the conversation.

"Yep. Know anything about it?"

Tom didn't like Kane too well, a fact he tried to cover up, because he had no real reason to have a bad feeling about him. It was just that Kane was so good at everything. He was one of the best left-handed pitchers in town, was impossible to guard in basketball, and guys who had played golf with him said he was pretty good at that, too. It wasn't fair.

"Spring Cotillion's worth a million, got to go to Spring Cotillion," yelled Motor-Mouth.

Williams put his hands over his ears.

"That guy doesn't talk," he said. "He vibrates!"

"I almost went to it last year," Kane said, his hands on his hips. He looked thoughtfully at the ground. "I was going steady with this chick who would have taken me to it, but we—well, she kept calling me all the time so we had to break up. It was beginning to affect my drop-ball."

Some guys, Tom thought wearily, think of nothing but getting on the diamond. All they think about is baseball.

He heard a small sort of "beep" on a horn, and turned around. Valerie Gates was right behind him, in a big car. Tom was so startled for a moment that he couldn't even tell what kind of car it was.

"Hi, Valerie," he said, and went on over to her.

She smiled at him. She certainly was very good looking. The car was good-looking, too. Black leather bucket seats.

"You'll want to drive," she said. She moved over and indicated that he was to take the driver's seat.

Tom nodded as he got in. He could feel the guys staring at him. They weren't saying a word; even Motor-Mouth was absolutely still.

He turned the thing around, called out to Williams that he'd dig him later, gave a short wave to the others, and drove off. It was more or less like a dream. He could hardly believe it.

"I don't like this big old thing," she said. "It's my stepmother's car. My wheels are in the garage. I bashed the front on a stupid tree."

"Bashed the front—how?" he asked, without thinking.

"Oh, never mind. You sound like my dad. You'd think I'd totaled the stupid thing, but I didn't. I've never totaled a car."

"Well, good for you."

This Valerie, Tom found himself thinking, must be one spoiled chick. But the fragrance of her perfume, or maybe it was only cologne or hair spray—he didn't know about such things—floated over to him, deliciously.

"You smell better than a new car," he said, sniffing.

"Ha! I like that!"

She picked up his notebook and screamed.

"'Unsafe to open at speeds exceeding 250,'" she read. "I love it!"

It was really a dumb thing to have on your notebook and he didn't know why he'd put it there. He'd seen it on the window of a drag car once.

"I love it!" she said again.

Tom turned on Seminole, one of the main streets, making a careful "driver-school" turn. This was an area of high-rent apartment houses with white statues gleaming on lawns, and swimming pools glittering through the trees.

There was a silence, and he knew he ought to say something.

"I really like your pool."

She giggled. "It was so neat, the way you dived off our sun deck!"

"That was maybe a little rank," he said.

Tom was relieved that she wasn't even mentioning the remark about the book he had mistaken for a rock group.

"Valerie—this party . . ."

He had found out most of what he needed to know about it, but was giving her the chance to say more.

"A lot of kids from Hoover go," she said. "They won't all be from Field. You'll know most of the people."

The strange thing was that her voice sounded a little limp, as though she wasn't too enthusiastic about it. She seemed almost sad.

"Do you really want to go to it?"

"I don't want to *not* go."

He could understand. The kids she knew were going. As far as Tom was concerned, the party was just a chance to be with her. He hoped that they could have some real dates, later.

"What I *would* like to do right now is to go to your place and see your drag car up close," she said. "Please!"

"Well . . ." He had to go to a record shop to get Lion's graduation gift for Robie, and besides, he felt a little uneasy about taking her to his house. "Could I get this gift, first? I did promise my brother I would."

"Oh, sure."

~~He took~~ the by-pass to Cherokee, because that was where the record shop was. Cherokee was also where the drive-ins were, and the automatic car-wash places, and the Parts Shop, and a store which sold motorcycles. There were people who spent most of their time cruising up and down Cherokee among all these various places. He found Robie an album he knew he would like. Tom already had his gift for Robie: zodiac cuff links with his sign, the sign of the crab; and Bonnie was making him a leather bookmark.

"What is it you call your car?" Valerie was asking.

"Purple Haze."

"I want to see Purple Haze."

"All right," he said, and headed for home.

"School was so stupid today," she sighed. "We had this stuff from the newspaper and a film." She sighed again. "We're supposed to be just fascinated by urban renewal."

"Urban renewal?" Tom used a question mark in his voice. He had discovered that if you say something in a certain tone of voice, you could sometimes find out what a person was talking about.

"You know. Cleaning up the slums and all."

Well. So they discussed the same things at Field that were discussed at Hoover. His school was not so different from the one attended by the great Miss Gates. But, as he turned down their street, Tom was uncomfortable. What would she think of it?

He was hoping, of course, that no one had dumped anything anyplace. As they started down the street it looked fairly good except that there were a few beer cans along the edge of the road. It was almost impossible to keep up with those cans.

"This is Budweiser Boulevard," Tom said, waving a hand like a big shot on TV.

"I like it, Tom!"

She probably thought it was all pretty gross, but she'd never say so.

"You might say this is *suburban* renewal," he went on, as he started up their driveway.

"This is really nice!" she said.

The ravine did look very pretty that day. They had put in a few bulbs the year before, and there were tulips blooming under the trees.

A brand new white Nova was in front of the garage. Robie's graduation present! And there was Robie, and also Mary. They had just picked up the car.

Tom got out and opened the door for Valerie, and introduced Valerie and Robie. Valerie already knew Mary, from Field. She rushed by her to look at Purple Haze.

"Take me for a ride!" she said.

"*Valerie,*" he sighed.

Even a girl like Valerie was rather dense when it came to C Modified Production. Tom had to explain, all over again, that you could not drive a racing car on the streets.

"All right." She nodded. She looked into the car. "Why, it has a wooden steering wheel!" She stared. "It looks like . . ."

"It's mahogany," Tom said. That wooden steering wheel was the most boss thing about Purple Haze. It was all that was left of Williams' old car. He'd sold most of his parts but had given them the steering wheel because he said he couldn't bear to sell it, and he knew they'd always wanted one just like it.

"That's great." Valerie said. "Everything else about the car is cold and precise, but you have a steering wheel that's carved and silky looking, like a nice table."

That was quite a thing for her to say.

"A friend gave it to us." Tom explained about it.

"A friend." She stared at him. "I don't have a friend."

"Come on!"

He just plain didn't believe her. She was good-looking, and Mary, who was not good-looking at all, had friends. It didn't figure.

"I'm—glad you like the steering wheel."

"How did you get it *on?*" She smiled and sort of lit up again.

"Get it on . . . oh, we put it on. My brother and I put it on."

She looked thoughtful. "You put it on. Yourself. Tom, you do things yourself. I don't do anything myself; I think that's why I get so bored."

Tom didn't see how a girl like Valerie could ever be bored. It seemed to him that there was something special, hard to describe but special, about her. Her talk about not having a friend was just talk, of course, and the strange thing was that she wasn't going steady, or something.

He had never known anyone quite like her. He did not feel that he was unused to girls; he had, he remembered, first gone steady in the sixth grade, and although he was through with the going-steady bit (much too complicated!), he generally had a date sometime during the weekend. But Valerie was super.

"What's happening!"

Williams, Motor-Mouth, and Kane came racing up the driveway.

"Hear Step has a new car!" yelled Williams.

"A *white* car, the *right* car, outa *sight* car—" Motor-Mouth was sounding off as usual.

"Not bad," said Kane. He was always so superior. "Not bad."

They were not only there to see the new car, Tom realized, as he made introductions; they were curious about Valerie Gates. He knew that they were impressed because Williams didn't even bother to hit him, and Motor-Mouth was silent for almost an entire minute.

"Fabulous!" called another voice, and Bonnie came running up the driveway.

"My little sis," Tom explained. "This is Valerie."

"How-do-you-do," said Bonnie. "Guess what, the school is going to produce my play. Excuse me, please, while I find Viola Bloomer."

"Who is Viola Bloomer?" asked Valerie.

"A cat," said Mary. "C'mon, Valerie. Let's get some cold Dr. Peppers for everybody; Robie has some."

"He does?"

"Yep. He has his own little refrigerator there in the back hall." She took Valerie's hand.

Mary was too thin and had to wear glasses, but she was the kind of person everyone liked, Tom thought.

The two were soon back with cold drinks. They sat on the cars, talking and laughing; Williams had found Robie's old bicycle and was trying to do "wheelies" on it; Motor-Mouth and Kane were wrestling.

"Wild!" Bonnie said, streaking out of the garage to join them.

Tom noticed, suddenly, that Robie was sitting there as though he were all by himself. His chick was there, his friends were there, and his brother and sister; well, his half sister and stepbrother, really, but they were his family; all these people were there, celebrating with him. *The Lonely Crowd*. Maybe the title of the book Mr. Ellers had been reading wasn't stupid, after all. There were people all around Robie, and yet he was alone.

Chapter Six

THE ENTIRE NEXT week was a down, for Tom. Grades were out and his mother was furious with him, and he was to be grounded until Friday. This was a real worry. How could he go to Spring Cotillion if he were grounded? As if that weren't bad enough, Lion called from Southern A and M and said, "You've got to learn to study! You have to book in college, I guarantee." Bonnie had reminded him that she hadn't missed a spelling word since the second grade, and Robie had also had a few words to say. Tom was surprised that Viola Bloomer hadn't expressed herself, with everybody else sounding off. Viola Bloomer sneered.

He felt so low one night that he spent the entire evening washing, waxing, and vacuuming Purple Haze. It made him feel a little better to get the drag car in good shape. There was talk that the speedway might be open that summer for grudge-racing, and he could at least look forward to that.

The night of Robie's graduation was the worst one of all. Even thinking about summer and racing didn't help. Everyone had their gifts for Robie, and Mary was there for dinner with her gift, and Bonnie had made a leather bookmark for him "because if you make your gift, it really means love." But Brian did not call or come. That was all Tom could think of, throughout dinner and all during the graduation ceremony—that Brian had not come.

"And Tom, I know he's right here in town," Tom's mother said to him, when they had gotten back from the auditorium and Robie had gone off to a party with Mary. "My boss saw Brian up at TenKiller, fishing."

He had seldom seen his mother this upset about anything.

"Mom, it isn't your fault," he said. "You fixed a nice dinner, and we all were there—you did the best you could."

She nodded, sighing. Then she changed the subject.

"You have a date for Friday, don't you? For some dance?"

"Well, yes . . ." He had even gone ahead and rented the tux, in the hope Mom would relent and let him go.

"I guess if you've accepted an invitation to a party you'd better go ahead. You do want to, right?"

He nodded. He wasn't really enthusiastic about the party, but he did want to see Valerie again. He had talked to her several times on the phone, but he hadn't seen her since the day they had all sat around on the cars.

"Then you go, Tom." She sighed again. "There's enough agony going on around here without my adding to it."

Friday night Tom was standing outside Valerie's house knocking at the front door and trying to keep from shaking. He couldn't imagine why he was shaking. He had been to parties before!

He looked down at his white jacket and at the fancy pants with a stripe down the side. The only person who could have made him rent an outfit like this was Valerie Gates. Valerie, he thought, ringing the doorbell. He even liked saying her name.

Valerie opened the door. She was wearing a long white dress, and he could smell her perfume.

"Hi!" she said. "Well. Is everybody still hacking at you about your grades?"

"Yes," he said. "But I can't understand why. So I got some D's. They were very *high* D's."

She giggled.

"Come and meet everybody," she said.

Tom tensed when he saw the big room full of people talking and drinking highballs. Her father was a big man with a booming voice. Tom had always been interested in other people's fathers. Beside him was a tiny lady with crisp white hair; Valerie's grandmother.

"Val didn't tell us how handsome you were!" she said. "Would you look at him, with those long eyelashes and that lovely complexion!"

"I'm glad to meet you," Tom mumbled, since you were supposed to be polite to older people even when they were gross.

"We're so glad you could come, Tom." This was

from Valerie's stepmother, soft-voiced and fragile looking.

"Would it be too drastic to have you and Valerie drive out to the club with us?" her father asked. "That way—"

"Daddy, no!" Valerie squeaked.

"That way," her father continued, "we can all arrive together, and then later, we'll bring you back here, and Tom can pick up his wheels and you can go to the after-party."

Tom said that would be fine. He liked Valerie's father. Mr. Gates said "wheels" for car, which sounded sort of funny coming from an older person, but he liked him anyway. It was just as well, too, that they were all going out there together; he would have no idea where to park at the country club, and sometimes Motor-Mouth and Kane worked out there parking cars; that would have been embarrassing, to have some guy you knew come up to park your car for you.

The first thing that struck him after they arrived at the club was how beautiful it was. And Valerie was easily the prettiest girl there. She had to have her picture taken with the others, before the dancing, and she was holding a huge bunch of roses. They almost hid her. Tom had a sudden feeling that she wasn't liking any of it.

But that place! He would have to remember everything about it to tell Bonnie. And he could just see Bonnie going to a big party some day, all dressed up with her hair fixed fancy; not this particular party, perhaps, but one like it, or a prom. The colors were white and pink and gold, and he could hear music starting.

He stood there waiting for Valerie and thinking

about parties. Most of the ones he had been to had been casual. In fact, they had been *very* casual. At the last one some guy had claimed Tom had shot him out with his chick. He'd jumped Tom, and if Lion and Williams hadn't moved in when they did, that cat would have killed him.

This was different—no fuzz—unless they were hiding. He didn't even see any dopers around.

"Stupid party," Valerie muttered as she joined him. "Stupid boring club."

He stared at her. Of course, she'd been coming out to this place all her life. It was nothing special for her.

"How'd you know that you were supposed to wear a tux?"

It took him by surprise. "What did you think I'd wear—cut-offs?" Had she thought that he would embarrass her by coming out to a dance at Southwest in old clothes?

She just looked away and didn't answer.

It was like that during the entire evening. Tom could have had a great time, the music was so good, but he could see Valerie wasn't having any fun at all. She seemed angry, and after a while he became a little hot himself.

While they were having some punch he asked her what was wrong.

She just shook her head.

"I'll tell you what's wrong, Valerie," he said. He was really hot, now, and he was also figuring things out. "I'm dressed like everyone else, and acting like everyone else. You're finding out that I'm just a straight cat. Which I guess I am. Sorry."

She gave a funny little giggle and for just a second she looked—ugly. Old and ugly.

"Valerie," he said, "if I'd come to get you all greasy and dirty from wrenching, you'd have liked it. If I'd come banging up in the Haze, you'd have thought it was great. If the fuzz had been on my tail, you'd have loved it."

He must have really called it the way it was, he decided. She looked startled.

"Tom," she gasped. "I'm sorry."

"You are not sorry," he said. "Do you think just because I dig racing and cars that I'm a bum? Is that what you thought?"

He didn't know why he asked her that, but he knew that it was true. "I can figure this out," he said. "I am not a complete dummered."

"Tom," she said, and she looked really shook. "Don't be mad. Please don't be mad. I don't want to hurt your feelings. Tom—"

The music had started again, and he couldn't hear her.

Valerie's grandmother beckoned to her to come over and meet someone, and Tom was left alone. He stood there watching the party and wishing he were somewhere else—anywhere else.

Valerie's father walked by a couple of times saying things like "Treating you all right, boy?" and "Everything okay?" He looked worried. Tom could feel it.

Then, suddenly, Mr. Gates was standing right in front of him, and there was an entirely different look on his face. Tom knew that he was really upset, and that this was serious. *Something's happened at home.*

"Tom," Mr. Gates said quietly. "Your stepfather,

Brian Smythe, has been killed in an accident in California."

All he felt was relief. *That's terrible. I feel relief. Not Mom, then; not Lion, or Bonnie, or Robie.*

"In California?" he asked, feeling that it was a dumb thing to say, not caring. "I mean, the last I'd heard, Brian had been here in town—"

"He was here, true. But he'd flown back to the West Coast today. He had been drinking heavily and lay down in a parking lot and a truck ran over him."

Tom was grateful that Mr. Gates was giving it to him without any fancy coverups or explanations. *Run over in a parking lot. Crushed to death.* As little as he'd liked Brian, a sickening shudder clutched at his middle.

"What's the matter?" Valerie had come running up.

"Just a minute, Valerie," her father said. He was still looking at Tom. "Your mother called. She is, of course, upset."

He nodded. If you'd ever cared enough about a person to marry them, you'd have to be upset at their death.

"This man's son—he would be your stepbrother?"

"Right," he said. "Robie. He lives with us."

"Your mother said that Robie is taking it hard. The news came over TV and they saw it. There was a picture of Brian Smythe, taken here at one of the lakes, and then the account of his death."

"Oh, that's terrible." Valerie was whispering. "That's so terrible."

What was terrible was that Robie probably knew, now, that his dad had been here and had not bothered to get in touch with him. That was what got to Tom.

And now, of course, Brian would never get in touch with Robie, or with anyone, again.

"I'll take you home," said Mr. Gates. "You'll want to be with your family."

"Thank you," he said stiffly. *This can't have happened.* It had happened.

Tom told Valerie that he was sorry that he had to leave, spoke to her stepmother and grandmother, and then left with Mr. Gates. A TV-radio news truck stopped them and a reporter tried to ask questions but Mr. Gates got rid of him in a hurry. He certainly knew how to handle things in an emergency.

"I'm terribly sorry about this," he said on the way back to Tom's house. Then he rather surprised Tom by saying, "I knew Brian Smythe. I knew his father and grandfather. They were fine people. Old 'Bry' Smythe was in on the original Wrenn Pool. I understand they took in a thousand dollars a day, for a while, from those oil wells. But he was more than just a millionaire." He paused. " 'Bry' was a fine man," he repeated.

"Then why . . ." Tom started to ask.

Mr. Gates shook his head.

"Who knows? Brian Smythe never had to lift a finger. He was sent to the best schools, got a new car with his driver's license, could sign a chit at any club in town. Maybe he had too much, Tom. He always struck me as a lost sheep."

They didn't say anything on the rest of the way home. Tom was mulling over a lot of things, and maybe, he thought, Mr. Gates was, too.

Tom asked to be let off at the end of his street. Mr. Gates didn't argue about it or ask why; just let him off and listened to his thanks, and left. Tom wanted to walk down the street and up the driveway and try to get his bearings. As he went up his circular drive he could see, through the window, his mother sitting on the couch holding Bonnie. It looked as though Bonnie was crying. She had never been the kind who cried much, but she was crying now.

He went in quietly, and then, gritting his teeth, hurried to his room. He dreaded facing them. His clothes were hot and sticky; he peeled off his suit coat and hung it up, and got off the tie and shirt and cummerbund, and the fancy pants with the stripe down the side. After fixing everything carefully on hangers, he pulled on jeans and a T-shirt and went out to the living room.

Bonnie was sobbing, quietly, "Well, he was my daddy. He *was* my daddy." She sounded puzzled. Bonnie had seen less of her father than Robie, he thought. *Brian's just been a name to her.*

Tom went over and hugged her, and hugged his mother.

"Where's Robie?" he asked.

"He took Mary home," his mother said. "Mary was here with us, until just a moment ago."

There was a sound at the door and footsteps; then they stopped.

"Robie?" she called.

Robie walked slowly into the room.

Tom went up to him and said, "I'm sorry, man."

Robie didn't answer.

Tom grabbed him by the shoulder. "It's—rough. I'm sorry."

Robie nodded. His face was as expressionless as

the dummies in the window of the tuxedo-rental store. He went over to a chair and sat down. Bonnie ran to him and crawled on his lap, but he still said nothing. He could not even talk to Bonnie.

His mother seemed fairly steady, now. She had probably cried all the tears she was going to cry for Brian long ago.

"Tom, do you think that you could manage here alone for a few days?"

"Why, yes. Sure, Mom."

"You could stay with my sister."

"I'd rather stay here. What's the plan?"

His mother began explaining that Robie wanted to go "to the service," and she had already been in touch with the California aunts and cousins, and that she would be leaving with Robie and Bonnie the next day. She'd even arranged for a week of her vacation. Tom had the feeling that the whole plan wasn't too convenient, but that she couldn't bear to see Robie take off alone.

Bonnie started crying again, so Tom went and got her and held her on his lap. Little kids like Bonnie were so soft, he thought, and yet you could feel their bones. He hugged her.

"We may be gone a whole week," his mother said. "And Lion will be taking his exams."

"I'm staying here," Tom insisted. "I can manage by myself."

He didn't want to bring it up right then, but he knew that the minute the place got a deserted look people would start dumping stuff all over the street again. He felt a responsibility.

"I'm not a baby, you can call me every day, and

I'll be all right," he said gently. You got no place with his mother if you yelled at her.

She nodded, finally. She agreed.

Robie went to his room to pack, and Tom followed to see if he could help, but of course Robie didn't want any help. He knew right where his suitcase was and his clothes were always in order. Tom stood there, in that neat square room, with nothing on the floor or under the bed, and stared at the desk with the bulletin board hanging above it labeled "My Future." Several more letters were now pinned to the bulletin board. "Sure you don't need any help?"

"Sure."

It was just then that Tom remembered he'd left the Chevelle in front of Valerie's house.

"Say, I've got to go get Mom's car . . . it's at the Gates' house . . ."

"Would you like me to run you over there in my car?" Robie asked.

He was folding shirts. He didn't even look up.

"Thanks . . . say, why don't we walk over there together?" Tom asked. He thought maybe it would be a good idea for Robie to get out and walk a little, as a release, and that perhaps as they walked along he might want to talk about things a little, or just be with him.

"I don't believe so."

"Why?"

"It's been raining," Robie said. "It might be muddy."

Well, Tom thought, I made the effort.

He got the car keys and told his mother and Bonnie that he would be back in a minute, and started off. It had stopped raining and was just misting a little, and a few drops fell on his face as he ran down the street. The air had freshened and felt good.

Quite a few cars were clustered around Valerie's house, and Tom was relieved that he had left the Chevelle out on the street. He was just starting to get into it when he saw Valerie standing at the top of her driveway. She had changed into jeans and a shirt, and as he stared at her she started toward him.

"Hi!" he called, and ran up to meet her. He was thinking that she wasn't so bad after all; she had come out to see him and express her sympathy.

"I'm sorry I had to leave," he told her. She looked great, he was thinking, even in jeans. "But you know why."

"Yes," she said. "It's so awful."

She hadn't blown up when he'd more or less deserted her at the party, either, Tom realized. She'd been spoiled a little by her folks, but she was all right.

"Your father was great, Valerie. The way he told me, without any fancy stuff; and the way he got me right home."

"I know." Under the politeness in her voice Tom now heard an edge of impatience. She paused, turning restlessly this way and that. "Well, I see you're all ready for the Barbecue!"

All ready for the Barbecue.

Tom was so startled he couldn't even speak for a minute.

"Ready for what?"

"The Barbecue!" She flipped her hair over her shoulder and looked up at him. "The *fun* part of this thing. The Committee wanted to have a fancy midnight breakfast at the Club, but we insisted on a different kind of after-party. Several of the kids have met here, because we were going for a dip, but it's too cold."

She paused. Tom stared at her.

"It's too cold," she repeated. "But in just seconds we're going to take off for this place for a barbecue, and—why, what's the matter, Tom?"

He could think of nothing to say. *Can't she guess that I'm in no mood for a party? What's the matter with her!*

"Well?" she asked. "What is it; are you still mad at me?"

"No," he said. "I'm not mad at you."

"Well?"

"Valerie! This man died. He was married to my mother, once; he was in our family; he was Robie's father. You met Robie. You met my little half sister." And, actually, he was thinking that perhaps she didn't understand all that. He'd barely mentioned Brian Smythe to her.

"But he was just your stepfather!" she said. "If he were your real father, I could see why . . ." and her voice trailed off.

He hesitated, not knowing quite what to say. "Look; a sad thing has happened at our house." He stopped.

"I don't understand!"

That was just it. She didn't understand. She didn't want to understand.

"Valerie Gates," he said sadly. She was beautiful and soft-voiced and shiny. He had liked being with her and sitting beside her; he had loved just saying her name; she was nothing.

Tom turned and walked down the drive.

If she had called out just once, he thought; called out his name and said just one real, honest, caring thing—*one*—he might have turned back to her.

She did not call.

Tom did not turn.

Chapter Seven_____

THE NEXT MORNING Tom drove the family out to the airport. He was getting constant instructions from his mother, who was looking rather tense because she had never gone away and left him before.

Robie didn't say much.

Bonnie had perked up because this would be the first time she'd ever been on a plane, and she had always wanted to go somewhere on a plane. Bonnie was also giving him instructions.

"Now, if Viola Bloomer howls to get in at night be sure and get up and give her a grape jelly sandwich on rye bread. That's what she likes. I always keep some rye bread in the freezer for her."

"If you think for one minute that I am going to get up in the middle of the night and fix a sandwich for a stupid *cat*—" Tom said. He was having enough trouble anyway, at that moment, trying to find a place to edge in among the taxis near the right door at the airport.

"You mean you won't?" Bonnie said, puckering up. "Tom!"

"All right, all right, I will!" If getting up at night and letting the cat in would make Bonnie feel better, he'd do it. "Don't worry. I'll make the sandwich. Viola Bloomer and I will get along fine."

He finally found a place near the curb.

"Just let us out and go, Tom." His mother's voice was insistent. "I have a feeling that Lion may be back at the house, by now, wondering where we all are."

"But Lion doesn't know what happened," said Robie, getting out in his slow, methodical way, holding the door open for the others. "Does he?"

"He's probably heard about it. Lion always seems to know things."

That was right, Tom thought. If he, Tom, "felt" things, had almost a spooky talent that way, Lion always knew things.

"Okay, Mom. I'll go right back home," he said. "I'll say good-bye here."

It started to rain as Tom drove away from the airport. He had never liked rain. What if Lion wasn't there? He dreaded the thought of going into the empty house. *But I'd better get used to it, I'll have a whole week of it.* His gloom increased as he got nearer home. Someone had dumped a fresh batch of beer cans near the entrance to their street; great. Then he saw the jeep in the circular drive. Lion was there!

"Hi, man."

He heard Lion's voice before he saw him. Lion had been in the garage with Purple Haze.

"Hi!" Tom jumped out of the Chevy. He could tell, by the look on Lion's face, that he had heard the news.

"It's rude," Lion groaned. "Rude!"

"Right."

"You think of how people hack at racers," he said. "Talking about how dangerous it is and all—which it can be—but we wear helmets, we're checked out before we run—we don't just lie down and get squashed!"

"The guy must have been drunk." Tom shook his head.

"How's Step taking it?"

"Not well. He's too quiet. It spooks me."

"Where are they all, by the way?"

"I just got back from taking them to the airport. They took off for California. Robie was set on going to the services for his father."

"That's strange." Lion looked around and shook his mop of hair. "Say, did Brian ever show up for graduation?"

"Nope." Tom groaned out the word. "He was right here in town, but didn't show. And Robie knows that. I should think he would be disgusted with his old man. So why go to his funeral?"

"Younger, it doesn't make sense."

"A lot of things don't."

He was thinking of Valerie Gates. She hadn't made much sense. She had made no sense at all.

"Have you had breakfast?"

"No. They were going to have breakfast on the plane. You don't have to bother about me. I can manage, and I know you've got exams, and all—"

"I got this one exam postponed until tomorrow. And you've got to eat, man!" Lion was jumping around and talking as fast as Motor-Mouth Murphy. "I'll cook breakfast. Besides, I've got things I want

you to do and I've got to clue you in." He propelled
Tom toward the house.

"Do?" he asked. "What—"

"On Purple Haze. I won't be through exams until
the end of the week. I have to lurk around school,
and *you've* got to get the Haze ready for the Points
Meet at Ringo." They were in the kitchen by now.
"Now, first you go out to Harley's, and—"

Tom had a feeling Lion was just planning things to
keep his mind off all that had happened, but that
was all right. He'd be glad of something to do.

As he talked Lion rushed around the kitchen, getting things out of the refrigerator. He seemed to fill
up the whole place. Before Tom knew it he was cooking bacon and mixing waffles.

"Lion, that's orange juice you're pouring into the
waffle batter," Tom said. "You're supposed to use
milk!"

"Oh?" Lion looked at the bowl, startled. "That'll be
all right," he said. "It'll give the waffles more flavor."

"I'll say this for your cooking," Tom said. "It has
flavor all right."

They had their breakfast, making a small waffle for
Viola Bloomer, and Lion finished telling Tom what he
wanted him to do on Purple Haze.

"And when everything's ready you're going to run
it, Younger."

"*Run* it!" He'd never run it. "Where!"

"At Western. They're letting guys try out their cars
on the track at night, for practice."

"I had heard they might do that!"

"Mr. Pop had something to do with it. See, the place
is just sitting there, and might as well be used. So

Mr. Pop talked to the mayor, and he and some Diddle-De-Do-Gooder professor convinced everybody to co-operate, because it would keep guys from drag racing down Cherokee."

This was good news.

"It's the only time I ever heard of a Diddle-De-Do-Gooder ever making a sensible suggestion," said Lion. "Which reminds me; I'd better split for Southern and book for my Sosh exam." He got up and started carrying plates to the dishwasher.

I'm going to get to run Haze, Tom thought. He could hardly believe it.

"Mr. Williams is letting us use one of his trucks for two weeks," Lion said. "I've already talked to him about it."

"You did?"

"Right. You know, old Buck Williams is interested in racing, too, and he'll be your wrench. He's going into American Legion ball but he can't play ball all the time."

Tom carried the rest of the things to the sink, trying to take in all these developments. It would never have occurred to him to ask Williams' father for the use of a truck.

"The tow bar Williams used to use is right in the truck, so you're all set," Lion said. "And you'll have Williams helping, and maybe Kane and some of the others. Now, Younger, about making a run. Don't let the motor get too hot. No more than 7800 R.P.M. Remember; don't let it get above 7800."

"Okay." Tom nodded. "Okay."

Lion stayed just long enough to help clean up the kitchen and then left in the jeep. Tom stood outside and watched him out of sight. Then he heard the noise of another car; it was Williams.

"I hear you're my new wrench," he yelled.

It was not going to be such a bad week, after all.

The night he went out to the track seemed unreal, almost dreamlike, to Tom. Williams had brought the truck over and helped him load up.

"Kane'll be here to help too, Youngie."

"Kane?"

He felt a little uneasy. Kane had had the first taxi-yellow Camaro in town (there were a lot of them around now) and Tom had always felt that because of his car, and the fact that he was a pitcher, Delbert Kane was stuck up.

"He's all right. A good guy. I know he gets a little hot when he's out there on the mound and people are calling him 'the Jolly Green Giant,' but he's okay."

Tom nodded. If Williams thought Kane was okay, he was.

He was even glad when he saw the yellow car come down the street. Kane did, at least, have good taste in cars. And he was big and strong and didn't mind getting his hands dirty. He'd be good help.

They went out to the Speedway a few minutes later, and by this time he felt easy with Kane and was glad to have him along. Kane looked a lot like Lion, except that he kept his hair neater. Coach had a fit if you let your hair get too shaggy.

"I appreciate you letting me in on this," Kane said. "I dig racing. You'll have to tell me what to do, though."

That was a switch, Tom thought; he'd be telling someone else what to do.

It seemed strange to be at the track with no crowds, the refreshment stands all boarded up and quiet, the seats empty, and the colors of everything a little too green and too orange, the way things were at a night game.

"Isn't that Mr. Pop?" Williams asked.

That was who it was. Mr. Pop was helping out, explaining to people that they could put down their dollars and make their runs and be timed. More and more cars, all kinds of cars, were pouring in. Tom drove to the pit and they unloaded.

"Young*er*!" voices called out to Tom, as the cars went by.

"You sure know a lot of these guys," Kane said.

He did know a lot of them; mostly racers who had been at Alvad. There were some he did not know, too. Near them in the pit was a car called "The Rattler." He'd heard about that car. It was a Chrysler Dodge Super B Six Pack, and it was supposed to have upholstery with a snake pattern. The owner and his crew wore helmets with tiny rattlers painted on them. Had he brought Lion's helmet with him? For a moment he felt the sickening heat of panic; he wouldn't be allowed to make a run without it. Yes; there was the helmet on the seat of the truck.

"What's that funny-looking stop light?" asked Kane.

"That's the 'Christmas Tree,'" Tom told him, and explained about the starting lights.

When it was his turn to run the Haze, Tom put on his helmet.

He knew now why Lion always seemed so tense. You couldn't help tightening up, even though you kept telling yourself not to. It was close and stuffy inside the closed-up car. He fired it. He was off! Tom shifted; shifted again. He kept his eye on the tachometer just above the dash; he knew that he should shift into fourth when it registered 7200 R.P.M. The car strained forward. There it was—7200 R.P.M.; he shifted once more. All he could do now was ride out the run. He was almost at the finish line; he hit the brakes and let out the clutch. *I can't believe it's over so soon.*

Tom had to turn the car slightly to go back on the return road, and it surprised him that Purple Haze was harder to turn, in a way, than the Chevy. Every thing about running the Haze was just a little different than he had expected. You actually had to drive the car to get the feel of it.

"You did okay," Kane yelled, as he got out at the pit. "14.02."

Tom nodded. That was nothing to boast about but nothing to cry about, either. He'd take a few more runs and try to improve it.

"You did okay," Kane repeated.

"Thanks," Tom said. But he was wondering; will I ever be in a real race?

The next day Williams came over early with some sheet metal. Lion wasn't worried about the fact that there was daylight showing around the shifter, but Tom's feeling was that it should be fixed up better, if possible. It was a good day. They worked right through until early afternoon, and then Williams had to leave for practice.

Mary came over later. She told Tom that Robie hadn't written to her, which surprised him.

"Wouldn't you think he'd write, or call?" she asked,

puzzled. Then she changed the subject. Before he knew it, they were talking about Valerie.

"You'll find somebody better than Valerie," she said.

They were in the kitchen. Mary was looking around for the dirty pans Tom had hidden in various places, and scrubbing them up for him.

"You're so different," he said. "You're not like Valerie at all."

She smiled. She was almost pretty when she smiled.

"Don't get the idea that everybody who goes to Field is exactly like everybody else; people don't fit into those neat little slots, you know."

That was certainly true.

"Valerie is just a spoiled brat." Tom about shouted it.

"I've never been especially close to her, Tom." Mary was standing at the sink scouring a frying pan. "It's funny; when we were little, I remember that her mother—her real mother—would bring her these beautiful foreign dolls from a European trip, but she never liked them. She wanted what she called new toys. She wasn't satisfied with what she had; she always wanted something new."

Tom remembered how she had put down her big house with its landscaped grounds. She had liked only the brightly colored umbrellas on the sun deck; they were new.

"She always wanted something *different*," Mary said, in a puzzled voice.

It figured, Tom thought, painfully. *I was different. I was a new toy.*

"Of course . . ." He hesitated. "Her parents are divorced and remarried . . ." Was he trying to excuse her?

"Ha!" Mary clanked down the frying pan and looked at him. "My parents are divorced and remarried. It isn't that bad!"

Tom had forgotten that Mary was split level, too.

She leaned against the sink and looked at him.

"I don't mean that some things aren't rough. They are. But there are bonuses. For example; I have this older sister, well, she's my stepsister, really, but that's just the point; I don't think of her as a stepsister. I feel she's my sister. When everyone is having a big discussion about something she'll stop them and say, 'I want to know how Mary feels about this.' And she really does. I can tell. And she's about the only one who doesn't hack at me to wear make-up. Or nag at me to eat more because I'm thin." Mary paused, head on one side. "She accepts me."

Tom could see what Mary was driving at. You had to have someone who would take you as you were. Lion and I are like that, he thought.

"Everyone has to have at least one person," Mary went on, a little desperately. "At least *one.*"

They talked about Robie as Tom walked her home.

"He gets depressed," Mary said. "I don't think any of you realize how depressed he gets."

Tom was beginning to feel depressed himself.

"What was that!" Mary gasped.

A striped shadow had flashed by them.

"Just Bonnie's cat," he said. "She's a very unusual cat; she chases dogs."

"I never heard of a cat chasing dogs!"

"Well, did you ever hear of a cat who liked grape jelly on rye?" Tom asked, and went on to tell her about Viola Bloomer's nightly snack.

Mary laughed, and Tom was laughing as he left her. He knew, now, one reason people had pets. It gave them something to laugh about.

The house was quiet when he got back. It was too quiet, too full of shadows. Tom went around turning on lights. Viola Bloomer sneered at the window, and he let her in. He turned on the television. The news blared out: "Teenage boy takes death run down Linden . . ." He snapped it off. They were beginning to call Linden "Suicide Lane," just as they called Cherokee "The Restless Ribbon." Tom picked up the evening paper. "Youth Kills Self . . ." There it was again. He didn't know the boy who had committed suicide, but he was just his age. Tom wondered what had gone wrong that would make anyone do such a terrible thing. Maybe he'd had trouble with his chick, or was worried about going into the army, or hadn't made the college of his choice. No one would ever know, probably, what really went wrong.

The quiet seemed to deepen. Tom could hear the ticking of the clock in the kitchen, a sound he'd never noticed before. He got up and walked restlessly around.

It surprised him, the way he missed everyone. He wandered through the house and down the hall to his mother's room. Bonnie's Camp Fire Girl uniform was hanging up above the ironing board. He missed Bonnie as much as he missed his mom. He went back to the kitchen and even up to the loft; Robie's room. Everything was neat and bare. There was Robie's bulletin board labeled "My Future," where he had pinned his acceptance letters from colleges. Robie could apparently go to the college of his choice. No worry about that, anyway.

It was getting late. He locked the doors and turned out the lights, his thoughts not comfortable ones. He was really more down than he had ever been in his life. Even thinking about Purple Haze didn't help.

Chapter Eight

LION GOT HOME the day the family were expected from California, and Tom tried to talk to him about Robie.

"I know, I know," he kept saying. "I've been trying to think what to say to him about Brian's death."

"That's just part of it." Tom felt rather desperate. "For one thing, we've got to stop calling him Step."

"Why?" said Lion. "It's just a nickname, like me calling you Younger or calling Bonnie Bon Bon."

"It isn't like that—"

"Remember the time Bonnie cooked a Chinese dinner, and we called her Won-Ton all week?"

"Will you listen to me for a minute!"

"Okay, okay, if you don't want me to call Robie 'Step,' I won't. We've got a lot to do. This place is a mess." He looked around him disgustedly. "We've got to clean it up enough so that Mom can at least walk through it."

He was right, it was a mess.

"And I want to fire the Haze. How's she running?"

"Smooth as silk."

"Bet you loved running it."

"I did."

"Any troubles?"

"Well, I red-lighted the first time; that made me hot. The next time I did okay. Cut a 14.01. Nothing great."

"That's better than I did the first time I ran it. Well. You can tell me all about it tonight, while we get Purple Haze ready for the Points Meet tomorrow."

"Tomorrow!"

"Right."

Tom hadn't realized that the meet was the next day.

"And I want to fire her at least once, and take her around the driveway. But now—*here*." Lion handed him a broom.

They got out to the airport in plenty of time, and the plane was on schedule. Tom saw Bonnie coming out the entrance with a huge bag and ran to help her.

"Shells," she said, hugging him. "I've decided to be a marine biologist. I went to the beach twice and Marineland twice. Hi."

"I've missed you, Bon Bon."

"I missed you too. We saw these big old mother trees. I may become a lady forester!"

"You'll be something, Bon Bon, I guarantee."

His mom looked tired, Tom thought. He had never seen her look so tired. He hugged her.

"Where's Lion? Oh, there he is. I'm glad to see you two."

She didn't really look glad about anything. Maybe, Tom decided, she was just worn out.

"Hello, Youngie. Hello, Lion."

It was Robie.

"Hi!" Tom shook his shoulder.

"*Robie*." Lion came up to them. "I'm—sorry about your father."

Robie nodded. "The services were very nice," he said in a flat voice. "Very appropriate." He coughed, and then looked around. "I guess we go that way for the luggage."

He was limp, as he always was, thought Tom. If anything, he was limper than usual.

The trip home was dominated by Lion explaining to everyone that Purple Haze was in really good shape.

"I know we'll take Street Elimination sooner or later," he said. "I flat know it."

Tom could feel uneasiness in the car, as real as fog on a cold day or heat in summer; he could feel Robie's silence. Beside him, Bonnie was asleep, her head thrown back against the seat.

"There are guys who have spent five thousand on a car and it won't run like Purple Haze," Lion went on.

It had never irritated Tom before to have Lion talk about the car. He liked hearing about the car. But now, for the first time, it seemed to Tom that they had spent entirely too much time on a car.

"I liked my cousins," Robie said suddenly. "I may decide to go to a West Coast school."

"Eventually we want to re-do the interior in gray leather." Lion, who was driving, was frowning into the traffic.

"That car," sighed his mother.

"Robie's talking about going to college in California." Tom nudged Lion. They ought to pay a little more attention to what Robie was saying.

"Good," said Lion. He nodded, flapping his hair. "Did you like it out there?"

"I certainly did." Robie spoke in a dull voice, like a mechanical toy. "Of course, dormitory space is always the difficulty in getting into those schools. Dormitory space, and pre-enrollment."

"Drag racing *started* in California," Lion said.

Tom sighed. There was simply no way to bring Lion and Robie together. No way.

Mary was waiting for them in front of the house. She ran up to Robie the minute he stepped onto the driveway.

"Hello, Mary," he said.

"I'm so glad you're back!" She hugged him. "You're back!"

"Yes, I'm back," Robie said. He pulled away as she kissed him. "It's good to see you, Mary."

Tom was puzzled. Robie certainly didn't seem very enthusiastic about seeing his chick.

Bonnie had dashed off to find her cat, and the phone was ringing inside.

Lion picked up one of the suitcases and called out that he would get the phone, and rushed off; the rest of them were left standing there.

"Let's go inside," Robie said, passing a hand over his forehead with an uncertain gesture. "I forgot how hot it gets here."

Tom picked up a suitcase and followed his mother and Mary into the house.

"Coming, Robie?" he called.

"Coming."

"Just take my things down to my room, please," his mother said.

As he passed Bonnie's room he could see her flopped onto her bed with Viola Bloomer. The trip must have taken a lot out of her.

He went on to his mother's room. Mary and Robie were standing in the front hall, talking; he could hear their voices.

"So you really liked California," Mary was saying.

"Oh yes. Well. Guess I'd better unpack." Tom could hear his footsteps, receding. He was going to his loft.

Tom put down the luggage and went to the hall.

"What's wrong with him?" Mary asked. "Is he mad at me?"

"Of course not. Why should he be? He's tired from the trip. I guess they're all tired. Bonnie's sacked out already."

"I guess I'll go on home, then. Maybe I shouldn't have kissed him in front of everyone. Maybe I—" She turned and, before he could stop her, ran from the house.

"Mary!" he called.

She didn't answer. She hadn't done anything to make Robie angry! So she'd run up and kissed him—after all, they'd been going steady for two years. It was Robie who had acted strangely, as far as Tom was concerned.

"Robie, Mary cut out," he called.

"Oh, she did?" Robie didn't sound very concerned.

"She thinks you're mad at her."

Tom went slowly through the kitchen and up to the loft, tapping on the open door slightly before he went into the room. Robie always liked to have you knock.

"You hurt her feelings."

"Oh?" Robie was unpacking. He gave a pair of slacks a little flip, and then hung them up very neatly in his closet.

"I notice you had Purple Haze out in the driveway, pointed toward the street," he said, in a pleasantly conversational tone. "Is she running okay?"

"Yes. Fine."

Robie wasn't that interested in their car. He was simply changing the subject.

"I can't understand you being so mean to Mary," he said. "She's really a nice person." He was remembering the talk they'd had and how concerned she had been about Robie. Then he remembered something else.

"You didn't even write to Mary. Or call her."

"I wrote her," he said. "She may not have gotten the letter yet."

"One letter! Big deal!" Did he care about Mary?

"I may be more or less West-Coast oriented, now, since I've met my relatives," Robie said. His voice still had the flatness Tom had noticed earlier. "And besides that, I've been thinking; I'm ready for college, and Mary still has another year at Field."

Was he going to ditch her, just because she was still in high school! Tom started to yell at him, intending to use several of Lion's choice terms, but then stopped in bewilderment. *The guy is bent out of shape.*

"Tom?" His mother was calling him. "Tom, where are you?"

"Up here." He turned and went down to the kitchen.

"What's that truck doing at the side of the garage?" she asked.

"Mr. Williams has lent it to us for two weeks," Lion said, running past them to the garage. "He's letting us use it as a carrier truck, and we're racing tomorrow, at Ringo."

But the truck was not really what she wanted to discuss, Tom soon discovered, as she beckoned him into the living room. "Don't argue with Robie, Tom."

"Oh? Why not?"

"Come here."

He followed her down the hall to her bedroom.

"I have given up."

He felt as though a cold shower had hit him. She'd never said such a thing before. Mom was not the type who gave up, and she looked so tired.

"It's hopeless," she groaned, dropping down on the bed, and there were tears smudging her make-up. "So don't argue with Robie and make things worse."

"What do you mean?" he asked her.

"I mean what I said. Being with Robie this week was like living with a zombie. He doesn't care about anything or anybody, and there is not one thing I can do to help."

"I don't see how you can talk that way." Tom dropped down on the floor beside the bed. "You're just tired, Mom, you had to go to those . . . services, and you were staying with people you didn't know . . . were they mean to you? Did they put you down?"

She shook her head, her hair flapping.

"No, no. They were great. They couldn't have been nicer; they were marvelous to Bonnie. They were marvelous to us all. They were solid types. I guess Brian was the black sheep of the family; they hadn't even known where he was, when he—when the accident happened." She looked at him again. "You can't do anything about people if they don't care, themselves, what happens to them. I should have known that. I should have known, because I failed with Robie's father."

"You failed! That's a laugh." And he would have laughed, except that he didn't want to make her feel worse. "*He's* the one who failed."

"Brian had just started to drink too much when I met him. And no wonder, he'd lost his wife, couldn't seem to hang onto a job, was trying to take care of his sick little boy . . ."

"Robie was sick?"

"It was just that he cried all the time and wouldn't eat and couldn't sleep," she explained, calming down for a minute. "The child needed mothering. I took him right in and had him in better shape in jig time, just took care of him, and Brian seemed like such a sweet guy, and . . ."

She was crying again.

"His child needed a mother, and you boys needed a father . . . you were only six months old . . ."

Tom could see that the situation had seemed just right, at the time.

"But I couldn't stop Brian from drinking. And I've failed with Robie."

"You did not fail," Tom told her, and he was trying to think of something, anything, that would make her feel better.

"Robie was just telling me that he might go out to the West Coast," he said. "He really seems to dig his relatives."

"He's going nowhere." And then she whispered, again, "I failed."

Tom told her again that she hadn't, and then, because he was really worried, he announced that he was going to get Lion. He knew that Lion was outside; he could hear the Haze being fired.

She quieted down a little and Tom rushed off to get his brother. Lion was lying under Purple Haze on the driveway, just looking up at it, with his transistor blaring away beside him.

"Everything's all ready," he yelled at Tom. "She could take off right now. Everything's set. There are a few things we might check, but she's all set."

Tom turned off the radio.

"Listen, you—"

"Never mind. It's Mom. You've got to come with me right away. It's Mom."

Lion jumped up.

"You mean she's sick?"

"No. Not that. But she's just lying there on the bed, and—"

"She's just tired! Bon Bon's asleep, already."

"Please come with me. Please. I—"

Lion got up.

"Okay, okay." He washed his hands hastily and shook off his shoes as they went inside.

They went into the house and through the kitchen to their mother's room.

"Dinnertime," she mumbled. "You boys get some of those hamburger patties out of the freezer, and—" She paused. "Where's Bonnie?"

"Bonnie's okay," Lion said. "And never mind about food, Mom. You rest."

"But—"

Her eyes were starting to shut as she talked.

"You sleep," Lion said.

Tom slipped off her shoes, and Lion got a light blanket and put it over her. It seemed strange to be doing those things. It was the sort of stuff she'd always done for them. Then they went quietly out and shut the door.

"We'll wake her up, later, so she can undress and get her bath and all." Lion was frowning. "She is just tired, isn't she?"

"It's that," Tom said. "And Robie."

"Robie? Robie's just the way he always is."

"She thinks—" He dropped his voice—"she thinks he's a gone goose."

"You're kidding! He's all set! He's going to college in California!"

"He's not all set."

There was a commotion outside and Williams roared in, all suited up on the way to a game. Lion rushed out the back door and told him to park farther away around the drive.

Tom started to follow and then paused, glancing up into Robie's loft. He started upstairs. Robie had finally finished hanging up all his clothes and he was putting away his things in a drawer. As he crossed the room Tom noticed the way he walked. Stiffly. Mechanically.

Mom had done all she could for him, he thought; more than most people would have done. *But Lion and I—what have we done?*

"Hey, Robie," he said.

Robie paused.

"Why don't you put on some old threads and help us wrench?"

He looked around.

"It's way after six. It's after *seven*."

What he meant, Tom knew, was that it was time for dinner. At six, you eat. At ten, you go to bed. At seven in the morning the bell rings, and then you get up. That was the way Robie lived.

"We'll chow down in a minute," Tom said. "But look; Lion and I are going to Ringo tomorrow, to this Points Meet. We'd like you to go too. So—"

"Why this sudden interest in my wrenching?" asked Robie.

Good question.

"Well . . ." Tom was in deep water. "You seemed to really like watching those races at Western, that day. So I thought—"

"Thanks just the same."

He doesn't care about anything or anybody—Who had said that? His mother. And she was right.

Then Tom noticed that Robie had taken down all the college application letters from his bulletin board, the bulletin board labeled "My Future." That could be, of course, because he was hoping to go to California, but still it seemed weird for a space marked "Future" to be blank. For the second time in an hour Tom felt a chill hit him.

Robie turned toward him. "I guess I'll drop by Mary's for a minute," he said.

And with a look around his room, he left.

Tom looked around, too, and then noticed three envelopes propped up against the typewriter. One was labeled "Mom," one was labeled "Mary," and one was labeled "Youngie." He froze.

Robie wasn't going to Mary's. Tom knew exactly where he was going.

Chapter Nine

TOM HEARD EVERYTHING about him very distinctly, as though someone had turned up the sound on the TV; he stood there watching Robie go into the garage; he saw everything clearly, too clearly; then, as Lion fired the Haze, he couldn't hear a thing. He moved to the door. Robie gave Lion a little wave and went past him, and got into his Nova and started down the drive. Tom knew he must think of some way to stop him, but he couldn't seem to think or even move. Something terrible was going to happen. He *felt* it. He shook himself and ran out into the garage.

"Robie!" he yelled. "Come back!"

The sound of the Haze drowned him out; he couldn't hear his own words. There was no way he could stop Robie. No way.

Lion had cut off the motor and gotten out of the Haze; silence hit like noise. Tom's next thought was that he could, now, ask Lion what to do, and explain how mixed up and lost Robie really was; how desperate. But wasn't it too late for explanations? No time.

He ran to Purple Haze and jumped into it, fired it, and took off. Robie was going to Suicide Lane and he had to stop him, and this was the fastest car in sight. Lion and Williams, standing beside the truck, turned and stared as he went by, their mouths wide open with surprise. At any other time it would have been funny, but it was not funny now.

He turned onto the street and even with the noise of the car and the stones and dirt flying around him he could hear Lion yelling. He jerked on down the street. *Maybe I am out of my mind.* He couldn't possibly catch up with Robie because out on the main drag, where Robie had just turned right, there were several stop lights and the Haze might stall at those lights. The neighborhood was heavily patrolled; the fuzz would be all over him in no time, and before he could convince them that he was trying to stop somebody from committing suicide, Robie would be laying rubber down Linden.

He turned left.

It was after he turned that he knew exactly why he had done it and what he must do next. He could take a short cut and pick up the by-pass in just four blocks, go down it two miles, turn onto River Road, and with any luck at all could reach the end of Suicide Lane as Robie would come down it. He'd swing Haze around so that it blocked the street, and then jump out and hope. Hope and pray. He'd be setting up a road block. That, and something more. Robie might not care about being alive, but Tom didn't think that he would be able to smash into Purple Haze. He knew how much Purple Haze meant to Lion and to Younger.

Robie would forget his plan and stop.

The by-pass was always busy, but it was right after the getting home rush and before the going out rush, so the traffic wasn't bad, but an old lady in a pickup was right ahead of him wobbling all over the road, and he had a rough time passing her, and just as he went over Cherokee some men on cycles started weaving back and forth in front of him. Then he heard, or thought he heard, a police siren. He tuned it out. A big bus was in front of him, next. He wondered if he would ever make it to River Road. He *had* to get where he was going; had to make it to Linden before Robie did. In a way, it was like a race. It *was* a race, but Tom had never wanted to be in a race like this.

The bus was still in front of him. Tom felt as though he was in one of those nightmares you have when you keep trying to get somewhere and can't. He didn't dare pass the bus, because he was too near the River Road turn-off sign. He'd have to start slowing up, or he'd go onto that road too fast and land in the Arkansas River. There was the sign. He slowed up and went into the turn-off to River Road.

The coast was clear. As he swung onto the road he didn't have to shift, which saved seconds; he went past Mimosa and Maple; the next would be Linden, so he decelerated, again. There was Linden. Suicide Lane. He turned, cornering very carefully, the car jumping just a little. For one sweaty minute he was afraid the engine would die on him, but it didn't. He looked up and saw that a white car had turned from Cherokee onto Linden. This was blocks away. He swung toward the curbing, and then shifted into reverse, backing just a little so that Haze formed a road block, and stopped. The white car was a Nova. It was coming flat at him, so fast that it seemed to bounce.

He hit the handle and got out, and the next thing he hit was grass. He was safe on somebody's lawn. He looked up and thought *That can't be Robie.* The car was coming too fast to be Robie. But it was a Nova, and it had to be Robie.

Tom beat on the grass. He hoped and prayed.

Robie can't hit Haze. He just can't wreck Purple Haze. He'd watched them wrench on it for so long, he knew Lion had pumped gas for two summers to buy parts, he knew they were going to the Points Meet tomorrow . . . but would he think of that? If all he cared about was smashing himself up he could still do it; the Nova was bigger and heavier than Haze, and he could crash right through our car and wipe himself out on the viaduct or in the river.

Tom heard the screech of tires.

He didn't want to look up, but he did. The white car was laying rubber; it slid to one side; jumped. He heard himself yell; he didn't know he was yelling; the car stopped, a little sidewise, just inches away from the Haze.

For sixty seconds there was absolute silence. Nothing. No movement, no sound.

Then everything happened at once. First Robie moved; he didn't get out of the car or anything but he moved, jerking a little, and his hands were over his face. Two police cars arrived, one from River Road and one from behind the Nova, and then Lion and Williams came steaming up in the tow truck. A woman in the yard was jumping up and down, and some little kids were screaming; but all Tom could think of was *Robie stopped. He did stop.* He stared at him. *Robie's all right.*

Before Tom had a chance to feel anything more but blank relief a crowd was around him. A woman was shouting, the round faces of children were staring, and a fat man suddenly grabbed him and shook him "to see if your spine is broke."

It was weird.

"You all right, Younger?" said Lion, pushing aside the faces. He looked dazed.

"Hey, you okay?" It was Williams, brushing off the fat man.

"I'm fine," he said. "I just . . ." He would never, never in the world, be able to explain it.

"We know what you had to do," Lion whispered. "You had to stop Robie, and you did it the only way you could do it."

Lion was not stupid. He had doped it all out.

The three of them, Williams, Lion, and Tom, turned together to look at the policemen, and the policemen stared back. *We must make quite a group. Williams, all duded up to play ball, Lion, with his wild hair and greasy clothes, and me—*

"Which one of you was driving the drag car?" asked one of the policemen.

He hadn't had to explain anything to Lion, but he had plenty to explain to the police, and no idea of where to start.

"I drove it, sir," he said. He gulped and went on. "I had to. I'm sorry, but I had to. I was trying to prevent a—an accident."

The policeman reached out and shook his hand.

Tom couldn't believe it. The whole scene became dim in his mind, like scratchy old movie film. He knew that Lion, after he was sure there would not be an arrest, went over and got into the Nova with Robie and just sat there with his arms around him, not saying much. Williams was explaining to the police that yes, sir, we did have a truck; yes, it was right there; yes, we'd load up the drag car and get it off the street right away.

Policemen must not be the way you think they are. They knew what had been happening on Linden, and they knew exactly what kind of an "accident" he had been trying to prevent; they knew what he'd done.

There was apparently just one hitch. The police were worried about Robie, and it was plain to see that they were uneasy about going off and leaving him.

One of them kept saying, "We must get in touch with the boy's parents."

This gave Tom a sick feeling. It was no time to explain that Robie didn't have any parents except a stepmother. And his mom had been through enough; all she needed, right now, was to get a call from the police.

"We can handle this, sir," said Lion. He had gotten out of the Haze and was standing in front of the policeman, and in spite of his greasy clothes, Lion looked as if he could handle it.

"You and this other—" The policeman jerked his head toward Tom—"are related to that boy?"

"Of course we're related," said Lion. "He's our brother."

Chapter Ten_____

TOM DIDN'T START to shake until they were loading up Purple Haze. Williams was really doing most of the work, as Robie and Lion had already left to go home in Robie's car.

"Why didn't Lion come with us?" Williams asked, as they finished and climbed into the cab of the truck. "What's the deal?"

"Oh, he just wanted to go with Robie, I guess." Somehow, Tom didn't want to discuss the matter with a friend, even as good a friend as old Buck Williams. It was a personal and family matter. He braced himself against the back seat; he must stop this stupid shaking.

"Look at those guys clearing the crowd away for us!" Williams shook his head, his black brows a straight line across his forehead. "I'll never say a mean thing about the fuzz again. Never."

"Right." Tom felt better as they started off toward home.

Motor-Mouth was waiting for them on his cycle as they drove up the circular drive, shouting that they were late, the game was at eight, and Williams parked the truck and hurried off to get in his own car and make it to the game. He was looking a little dazed, Tom noticed. *We're all still shook.*

Just as Williams left, though, he yelled, "Good luck at Ringo, Lion!"

Tom had completely forgotten about the Points Meet.

The Points Meet was the *last* thing on his mind.

Lion hadn't forgotten about it, though, and as Tom walked into the garage he found that Lion was busily telling Robie about Ringo.

It was almost as though that wild half hour they'd just lived through had never happened.

"I couldn't smash your car," Robie whispered. "I couldn't do it."

"I know, I know. Now about this Meet—"

"I even remembered that you were going to race tomorrow."

"And we want you to go to Ringo with us."

"I don't see why—"

"Does there have to be a reason for everything?" Lion was almost shouting, as he did when he got hot about something. "We just want you to come!"

"Well, I . . ."

Lion was getting through to him, Tom thought. Lion could get through to anybody, if he put his mind to it.

"Do you really mean it?" asked Robie. "Won't I just be in the way?"

"No." Lion shook his head. "You can watch, at first, and then help. We really need a third man. Some people use more. This cat who runs 'The Rattler' has four. Four guys, helping him."

Tom was glad Lion was taking over. He wasn't feeling too good. Reaction, or something. He thought of the guy doing rail time, the one who had yelled, "I was about *lost*." Robie, too, had been about lost.

He went in the back door and leaned against the wall. Nothing was tilting, and he didn't feel faint, but he did feel that he was going to be very, very sick. What he would have liked to do was just cut out and go for a long, long walk somewhere, all by himself. Then he straightened up. He could not get sick. He simply could not. And he couldn't go for a walk, either.

There were things he had to do.

He checked to be sure that Robie and Lion were still in the garage, which they were, and then he went very quietly up into the loft and did something which he would not have ordinarily done. He destroyed the three letters marked "Mom," "Mary," and "Younger." He didn't read them.

Then he wrote a note to his mother. He didn't want to disturb her, and yet he couldn't bear the thought of her waking, in the morning, to find them all off to the Points Meet (because, from what he was hearing, they would be) and then discovering, through something in the paper or people telephoning, the thing which had almost happened to Robie.

"Dear Mom," he wrote. "Things are O.K. now. You'll see. We are taking Robie to the Points Meet with us, tomorrow. We'll be back about dinnertime. Love, Tom."

He went to her room with the note. He still didn't

wake her, as he figured she needed her sleep more than anything else, but put the note where she would see it the first thing in the morning.

Then he went back to the kitchen. There was one more thing he thought should be done.

"Robie!" he called.

Robie and Lion were now sitting on Haze, talking.

"Robie!" he called. "Go and call Mary. Please."

"Okay."

He went into the house and called her.

"Yes," Robie kept saying. "Yes, I know."

Lion and Tom walked out to the ravine and sat on a stone. It was dark and quiet.

"Younger . . ." Lion sounded shook. He was about as shook as Tom had ever seen him. "The only reason he's here is you. You saved him."

"I guess so," Tom said. He thought about that. "Or *you* did. Because just stopping a guy isn't enough. He could always try again. But you said, 'He's our brother.'"

He could hear Lion sigh.

"*Why?*" asked Lion. "Why was he so . . . *down?*"

They sat there without talking for a moment. Then Tom asked Lion something. "Would you say Robie is home safe, now?"

"I would not." He paused. "We'll just have to try and help him all we can."

When Lion woke Tom in the morning he couldn't believe that it was time to get up. He would have sworn he'd just gone to bed; it couldn't be morning!

Robie was already up.

"No, *no.*" Lion was talking to Robie, who was in a

nice crisp pair of slacks. "Here." And he handed him a pair of jeans, all faded to that nice shade of blue they get just before they start splitting. They were Lion's favorites.

They got dressed and went out into the hall, and Tom noticed that there was a light on in the kitchen. Their mother was up, fixing sandwiches for them. She must have awakened in the night and read his note.

"Hi!" She gave Tom a quick squeeze as he went by.

Yes, she had read his note. And she probably had some idea of what had happened, he decided. But she wasn't saying a word about it. She was a strong person. A thought struck him; it was not too bad, after all, to have white skin and green eyes.

Bonnie came trailing out with Viola Bloomer. "Presents," she said, passing out packages. She had gotten N.H.R.A. T-shirts for everybody; she'd bought them in California.

"For you too, Robie."

Tom hugged her. "You are the world's best Bon Bon."

"Aren't you going to put them on?" she asked. "Don't you want to wear them to the Meet?"

Tom told her no, they'd save them for dress.

"I suppose that some day you kids will want to do something besides wear your worst-looking clothes and fool around with cars." His mother now seemed more like herself.

Then they were off in the truck, and it was the way it always was before, going to a race, except that it was better.

"Everything looks so—new," Robie said, suddenly.

New? Tom was puzzled, and yet he could under-

stand. Robie had always stayed inside so much, booking, that he'd never noticed things like the way trees
and sky looked in the morning, and how nice morn-
ings were anyway; any morning. There were people
standing around waiting for their bus or their ride, all
pleased and eager looking instead of tired and beat,
the way they might be later. A guy on a cycle noticed
their rig as they paused at a stop light, and said "Hey!
Going to the Points Meet?" and when they said "yes"
he called, "Good luck."

Robie kept looking this way and that, enjoying it all.

The radio was on and Glen Campbell was singing
and for some reason the song was just right. Tom put
on his racing hat.

"What is that?" gasped Robie, suddenly. He'd never
even noticed his racing hat before!

"That's my hat. You *book* so much—" He paused. The
last thing in the world he wanted to do was to bawl
Robie out or put him down.

"Yeah?" said Robie. "Go on. What were you going to
say?"

Tom went on. After all, if he wanted to tell Lion
something, he told him. He didn't have to be so careful with Robie any more.

"I just mean . . . well, I don't want to put down
booking. I intend to do a little more of it myself,
from now on, but you need to get out and see what's
happening too."

Robie nodded, solemnly. And yet, Tom thought, he
wasn't looking as solemn as he usually did.

They had crossed Red Bud, and were in the country.

"You know," Robie said, "it's pretty out here."

"Sure it is."

Lion brushed a peacock feather out of his eye and said, "I thought you gave that hat to your chick."

"She gave it back. She's not my chick."

He didn't say any more, and Tom was glad he didn't, because he didn't want to talk about Valerie. He didn't want to even think about her. *Valerie Gates.* What was she doing, right now? Sleeping, in that big stone house she hated? Staring at a wall, unable to sleep? Or sitting out on her white sun deck, under one of the orange umbrellas? Someday he would be able to think about her, get everything all doped out.

". . . I know you could get into a much better college," Lion was saying to Robie. "Southern's just a state school, and not even the biggest state school, but it has a good Humanities department and this big old Fine Arts building, now, and some unreal professors. Good men. You might like taking your first two years there! And I know I could get you into our dorm."

Tom hadn't been paying attention. Now he was. Lion was getting Robie all fixed up at Southern!

"You want me in your dorm?" asked Robie.

"Sure! Sometimes we sit up late and have a real bull session about *everything*, and then I go out and get a six-pack and some frozen burretoes," Lion said. "You know that steam iron Mom gave me? I turn it upside down and cook the burretoes on it. It's just right when you set it for wool."

Robie threw back his head and broke up. "Steam iron . . . burretoes . . ." He couldn't seem to stop laughing.

He'll like being with Lion, Tom thought. *It may take him awhile to get used to it, but he'll like it.*

"Oh . . ." groaned Robie. He wiped his eyes with a

handkerchief. Then he straightened up. "Say, what about breakfast?"

"We'll stop at the Wagon Wheel," said Lion.

"We have to turn before we get to the Wagon Wheel," Tom reminded him. "We're going to Ringo."

"There's *always* a Wagon Wheel," Lion said. He jerked his head toward Tom. "May let you make a pass or so, Younger."

"Really?"

"Why not?"

"But I've never raced."

"The hell you haven't," said Robie.

Nobody spoke for a moment, and Tom was determined to not be the first to sound off and make himself out a hero.

"It's just that I feel things," he said, finally.

"Okay." Lion was sitting up very straight. "You *feel* things. You always have. What are our chances of taking Street Elimination?"

Tom snapped his fingers.

"No doubt about it," he said. "We'll win."

About the Author

Elizabeth Allen, though born in New York State, has lived most of her life in the Mid-West or West. She is a graduate of the University of Michigan, and her poetry and short stories have been published in several major periodicals.

This is her fifth published book about teen-agers, and she admits that the suggestion for "some kind of book about drag racing" came directly from her two sons.

The author and her husband, a surgeon, live in Tulsa, Oklahoma. They are the parents of a daughter and two sons.